# SKIN DEEP

## And Other Stories

## Suzi Hayward

# CONTENTS

# SKIN DEEP

'Will you stop looking at that guy,' Milly nudges me. 'It's freaking me out.'

She has a point, but I can't help myself. I sneak another quick look. There are five guys standing together at the bar. All of them "well fit" but the one with his back to me just aces it. He turns slightly and I see that he has lightly tanned skin and a fine profile. His hair's perfect as well – a gorgeous dark blond thatch, so reminiscent of a teddy's plush fur; I itch to rake my fingers through it. But dark glasses, come on, I can't see those eyes which I am betting are as sexy as hell. If only he'd take those sunnies off, I could get a proper look.

He's talking animatedly, and his mates are enthralled. One of them leans towards him, almost howling with laughter. 'Only you, Jed,' he splutters. 'Only you.'

So now I have a name. I ponder on the sobriquet. Short for Jeremy, Jared, Gerrard, perhaps. Jed suits him though; tough, cool, confident.

He'd walked up to the bar, oozing masculine charm, his tight jeans and blue silk shirt combo perfectly displaying a superb, toned physique. The guys at the bar had whooped with delight, vying with each other to get his attention. Life's great for beautiful people, they don't have to work as hard as the rest of us – as one of my mum's favourite songs goes, "summertime and the living is easy". Well, every day is summertime for some lucky sods.

'Bessie, if you're that interested go and introduce yourself and get us another drink whilst you're at it.' Milly drains the last of her Pinot with something resembling a slurp and hands me a tenner.

Well, *carpe diem* and all that. For once I'm going to seize the damn day. I pick up my purse and wander over to the bar, managing to squeeze myself into the space between Gorgeous Jed and one of his mates. It might be the two glasses of Sauvignon I've downed whilst gazing in wonder at Jed's back, it might be that for once I'm feeling like Miss Super Cool after the ministrations of Audra at New Face, but I am going to get to talk to Jed before I trot back to Milly, and what is the harm? I want to get a look at those peepers as well so that I can flesh out my fantasy of him when I replay the moment later tonight in my lonely bed.

'Ooh,' I exclaim, grabbing hold of Jed's sleeve. 'I just love your shirt. I've been wanting to get one that colour for my brother's birthday. I don't suppose you could tell me where you got it?'

Jed turns towards me, a bit disconcerting because now I can see the specs are of the mirrored-glass variety and usually I avoid mirrors like the plague. But then, wonder of wonders, I'm getting his full attention as he leans over and puts a hand on my arm. 'Thank you. I wish I could tell you, but I'm afraid this shirt was a present; but I must admit I do like the colour.'

'Now let me guess,' I say boldly. 'Does it match your eyes?'

Well, that works a treat because the next thing I know he's reaching up to take off his stunna shades and my excitement grows as I'm about to see those maybe baby blues, but then I take a step back in shock because there is only one eye, which is blue, but where the other eye should be there's just a deformed bulge with a dreadful grotesque jagged red scar running across it.

'I'm so sorry,' I manage to say.

I grasp the drinks and change from the bar and scurry back over to Milly. I am shocked but more than anything I'm so deeply ashamed of the way I just behaved. I wonder what Milly will make of it, but I realise she's looking at her phone and then she swears and thrusts it into her bag, and next thing she's swigging back half the glass of wine I've just put on the table and gathering her belongings together.

'Sorry, Bessie, babe, but I've got to shoot off. My mum's turned up and Jake can't cope with her. By the way, you look fabulous. Text you later. Bye.'

With that, Milly's off to deal with the latest "mum crisis" and I'm left sitting sipping my drink and trying to decide what to do. I've behaved badly but I need a few minutes by myself to regroup. I slug back the rest of my wine, grab my bag, and hurtle into the ladies. On the way past the mirror, I check my look. Apart from my startled expression, I look fine. Yes, Audra has done a fab job. My skin is smooth and glowing. For once my hair has behaved itself as well; long, sleek and blonde (with a little bit of help from the highlights and trim last week). I do look OK, but I feel shocked and confused. I take refuge in a cubicle and sit with my head in my hands. Jed's face was just so unexpected. Then I'm struck by an incredible thought. I know exactly what I'm going to do. 'It's fate,' I mutter to myself, 'gotta be.'

I make my way back to the bar. Unsurprisingly, Jed has replaced the glasses firmly on his head and he's talking away to his mates. 'Yeah, yeah, much as I expected,' he laughs. 'Only skin deep and all that.' He looks surprised as I approach.

'Look,' I say, 'I'm sorry I had to run off. I knew my friend was on a tight schedule, so …'

'Don't worry. It's cool.'

He starts to turn away, but I grab his arm. 'Hey, I'm feeling a bit awkward, my friend's had to leave and well, would you mind just keeping me company for a little while.' I'm starting to wobble now but he takes pity on me.

'Okay.' He tilts his head to one side, asking, 'You sure about that?'

I nod my head, half expecting scorn, but he leads me over to a table in the corner.

'Now, let's get you another drink, what'll it be?'

I opt for a spritzer and determine to sip it

slowly.

At first, I feel a bit uneasy, but Jed seems quite happy and relaxed. 'I'm Jed, short for Jedidiah,' he proffers a hand across the table. 'I was named after my great-grandfather who was Jewish, in Hebrew it means Beloved of the Lord.'

'Well, that's a sort of coincidence,' I say, shaking his hand enthusiastically. 'My name's Bessie. My mum loved her nan and wanted to call me after her, but she didn't really like her name. It was Elizabeth and mum thought that was a bit stuffy, so I got christened Beth, but over the years I became Bessie – possibly because it rhymes with messy.'

'You don't look messy. More immaculate, actually.'

'You should see me first thing in the morning,' I joke and then splutter on my drink because for me that sounds way too forward.

Anyway, apart from totally demonstrating my messiness, the spluttering completely breaks any remaining ice, and we start talking about families and discover that we do have things in common. We were both dragged up on seventies rock. My mum sang in a band for a while and Jed's dad was a semi-professional guitarist. We spend the best part of an hour talking music trivia and singing snatches of our favourite rock classics, and I'm almost getting to the point of telling Jed something else we have in common when he says, 'I don't for one minute suppose you'd be interested in coming back to mine for a coffee, would you?'

'That would be great,' I say, and the next thing we're walking back to his place hand in hand, which just seems natural and nice.

His flat is way smarter than where I live. 'Wow, you must have a good job,' I suggest.

Well, I get by,' he says. 'I'll give you three guesses what I do.'

As we'd walked along, I'd admired his aftershave, which had a sensual, warm, woody aroma and he'd said it was a sort of a perk of his job.

'Executive in a perfumery company, perhaps,' I say, laughing.

'Not quite right. You can have two more guesses, but maybe after we've had that coffee.'

Jed goes into the kitchen, and I sit down on the comfy sofa. I can't wait to tell him all about me. We were made for each other, and it was our destiny to meet. This is turning out to be the best day ever; surely the first day of our future together. He's still wearing the dark glasses. I hope he'll soon feel relaxed enough to take them off, maybe over coffee.

Feeling excited and restless, I have a wander round the room. On the bookshelf there's a large, framed photograph of someone who looks like Jed but minus the scar and with two lovely sparkling eyes. The photo looks familiar and then I realise I've seen it before on a poster advertising an expensive aftershave.

'Aha, you've discovered my guilty secret,' says Jed, as he comes through the door holding two steaming mugs.

'So that is you, I thought so.'

'Yeah, I do a bit of modelling – that sort of stuff mainly, but ...' He places the mugs on a small table and turns to face me, as he does so, removing the glasses and plucking at the lump where his eye should be and then he's peeling back the flap of skin and pulls it away, revealing a beautiful set of blue eyes and a perfect face.

I gasp in horror.

He laughs. 'Not quite the reaction I was expecting,' he says. He passes me the awful prosthesis. 'I always suspected that girls only liked me because of my looks, but you've proved me wrong and wow, it's a nice surprise. My mate's training to be a theatrical makeup artist and I was his model for the day. I promised the lads I'd show them the results.'

'I've got to go,' I stutter, flinging down the prosthesis and reaching for my bag.

'No, babe. Please don't go. You're beautiful. You could have any guy, but you didn't go for me just for my looks. You're genuine, you're wonderful. I'm so happy to have met you.'

I feel sick with disappointment. 'Look sometimes things aren't quite what they seem,' I say.

'Oh please, I wasn't trying to make a fool of you. I'm afraid when you asked the colour of my eyes, I just couldn't resist showing you what was behind the specs. It was mean and I totally deserved your response. When you came back, I was really surprised. Then I thought how good it would be to get to know someone who didn't take everyone at face value.'

That sounds more promising. Perhaps there is hope after all. I dither for a moment. Jed reaches out and grasps my hand.

'The last couple of hours has been fantastic. I really admire you. I know it's shallow, but I've never been good at coping with disfigurement or really physical imperfections of any kind. But you, well you're beautiful inside and out.'

'I need to use your bathroom.'

I pull my hand away from his and totter to the bathroom which is well-stocked with high-end male grooming products. I help myself to a swathe of cotton wool and a tub of cleansing lotion. Audra did a wonderful job with my makeup. I've never had such a good result with anything else I've ever used. It's going to make such a difference to be able to face the world with an unblemished face, but I don't think it will look so good in the morning. I might as well come clean now while there's still time to get the last bus home. I start to rub away my immaculate complexion and reveal the port-wine stain birthmark that covers half my face.

# PERFECT

Don was not a happy man. He used to look forward to Friday nights when he and Izzy would treat themselves to a meal and a few drinks at the Tipsy Toad whilst planning their activities for the weekend; but Izzy didn't seem to be bothered anymore. When they had first married her appearance was almost immaculate. Her beautiful dark brown hair was always clean and shining, her makeup carefully applied, her figure trim, and her clothes co-ordinated and spotless. It was a different story nowadays.

'You go on Don, I can't be bothered,' she had said that evening, and that just about summed her up as she had sprawled across the settee looking decidedly homely in her baggy track suit bottoms and grubby tee-shirt. Thus rebuffed, Don trudged along to the pub feeling dejected and rejected. At one time Izzy would have been delighted to accompany him, holding onto his hand and looking up at him adoringly. 'Can't be bothered,' he muttered to himself. 'Can't be bothered to look nice for me, can't be bothered to be with me, and definitely can't be bothered about me.' In their early years together, Izzy had always put his comfort first and deferred to his opinion but now her appearance was almost slovenly and her attitude sometimes downright stroppy.

The Tipsy Toad was buzzing and even though it was only early evening there were no vacant tables, just a couple of empty chairs on a table for four in the corner. One seat was occupied by an elderly gentleman stooped over a brimming pint glass. He was wearing a strange slightly crooked felt hat. Don thought he looked "a right weirdo" but it was the only space available.

'Anyone sitting here?' he asked as he pulled out a chair.

'No, my young friend,' said the man, smiling broadly and showing a rather repulsive mouthful of yellowing teeth. Don winced at the quaint turn of phrase, but he'd bought his pint now and he needed it. He sat down, wishing he'd got a paper to read. Never mind, he would down the pale ale swiftly and get off to the Miller's Arms. He assumed what he hoped was a blank expression to discourage further conversation but "the weirdo" had other ideas.

'You look a little glum my friend,' he offered.

Don sighed. He couldn't decide whether to completely ignore the man or make some non-committal response but before he could commit to either the stranger continued, 'woman trouble, I'll be bound.'

'Yeah, you could say that,' agreed Don reluctantly.

'Our spouses so seldom live up to our expectations,' continued the man. Don nodded.

'But perfection can be a terrifying thing. Now, given the choice would you really want a perfect wife who deferred to your every need?'

'Too right I would,' Don laughingly replied.

'So, if the opportunity arose to cast a spell on the fair Isabel to transform her into the woman of your dreams, would you do so?'

'Indeed, I would,' Don found himself saying. He suspected he would regret this and that he would be drawn into some mad rambling conversation. The fact that the stranger seemed to know Izzy's name puzzled him though. He looked more closely at the fellow in front of him but was pretty sure they had never met before. For one thing his accent was very strange, some sort of indefinable brogue, but he definitely wasn't a local.

As if reading his mind, the man thrust out his hand saying, 'No, you don't know me but let me introduce myself. My name is Wilbur and yours of course is Donald.'

Don wondered whether the man was some sort of acquaintance of his father or grandfather even. Yes, that must be it. The world could be a small place sometimes and there would be some logical explanation. He finished his pint and rose to get another, feeling obliged to offer a drink to his new acquaintance but this was declined.

'Not necessary, my young friend,' said Wilbur.

When Don returned with his fresh pint, Wilbur had taken out a small notebook. He was flipping through the pages and muttering to himself. As

Don sat down, Wilbur turned to him and smiled. *Those teeth* thought Don. *Couldn't the guy afford a dentist? He'd be better off with some dentures or something.*

Again, Wilbur accurately discerned his thoughts. 'You young, so concerned with outside appearances.' He shook his head. 'But no matter, tis your choice my friend and the choice you have because,' again he thumbed through the small notebook, 'I have two spells remaining for the month and only two days in which to use them. They can't be carried over you see.'

*Yes,* thought Don. *Completely mad or was this some weird and wonderful scam? Well, if it was money he was after he was definitely out of luck.* 'Sorry mate, I'm cashless nowadays and I'm guessing you don't have a card machine.'

Wilbur frowned. 'There is no charge, but the price may be high. Who knows? You may wish we had never met, so let me ask you again if you wish to use this spell to transform the fair Isabel into the wife of your dreams?'

Don decided to humour the fellow. 'Yes, go for it,' he said.

'It will be done,' said Wilbur.

He grasped Don's hand firmly and then finished his pint and arose from the table. Don watched him walk to the door. As he made his exit, he turned and saluted Don and then he was gone. Don bought himself another pint, stretched out his legs and settled in for the evening. *Izzy would be fast asleep by the time he got home, possibly still sprawled on the settee wine glass in hand. Oh well, she could stay there,* he thought.

Don was surprised that the house was in darkness. He went upstairs and, by the light of the bedside clock, saw that Izzy was already in bed, seemingly sleeping soundly. He climbed in beside her, casually throwing his arm around her. Her hair was spread over the pillow and surprisingly smelt clean and fragrant. She must have washed it before retiring for the night. He fell into a heavy sleep, the four pints of pale ale taking effect.

When he awoke the next morning, Don found he was alone in the bed. That was unusual. Izzy had got into the habit of sleeping in on a Saturday morning, usually waiting for him to make her an early morning cuppa before she stumbled out of bed to attack the weekend chores. He debated having a shower but then decided not to bother; Izzy probably wouldn't even notice. Slinging on his weekend wear of old jeans and sweatshirt, and feeling a little worse for wear, he trudged down the stairs and made his way to the kitchen. A delightful aroma of bacon and eggs, and fresh coffee greeted him. Izzy was turned away from him cooking breakfast on the hob. He was surprised to see that the table had been laid in the dining area, the cutlery carefully placed along with serviettes and a jug of flowers.

Don noticed then that Izzy's hair was loose and lustrous around her shoulders. She was wearing nicely pressed white jeans and a smart flowered top. She turned towards him, saying, 'Breakfast is almost ready darling.' He waited for a hint of sarcasm but there was none. Her carefully made-up face broke into a welcoming smile.

'Did you sleep well?' she asked.

'Well, you obviously did,' he said.

'Yes, I did, darling,' she replied. 'It's a lovely morning.'

Don looked in amazement as she poured him a cup of freshly brewed coffee. It was years since they had drunk anything but instant. He checked the date on his watch. No, it definitely wasn't anyone's birthday or an anniversary, and he was pretty sure he hadn't stumbled into the wrong house, although he wasn't used to seeing the kitchen in such pristine condition.

The meal was delicious, and Izzy catered for his every need, topping up his coffee and bringing fresh toast to the table. He couldn't get over her appearance; it was almost as though he had walked onto the set of an advertisement displaying the idyllic lifestyle of a modern couple. He realised that his appearance was the only discordant note, but Izzy didn't seem annoyed or offended. She continued to smile benevolently as he finished his meal, even handing him the newspaper and suggested that he go and relax in the lounge.

He opened the newspaper, and, almost reassuringly, it was filled with the usual grim news and fatuous articles involving minor celebrities. He could hear Izzy humming a happy tune as she washed the dishes and tidied the kitchen. She came into the lounge, telling him that she was popping to the supermarket to do a weekly shop and asking if there was anything he particularly fancied eating.

He looked at her quizzically. 'So, what is this, Izz?' he asked.

'What my darling? Is everything OK?' She looked concerned. He studied her for signs of sarcasm but could see none. In fact, he could see nothing wrong with her demeanour or appearance; not a hair out of place, not a crease in her clothing; her skin was smooth and unwrinkled. She even appeared to have shed the few extra pounds she had gained over the last few years.

She raised perfectly groomed eyebrows, saying, 'Is there anything I can get you before I go out?'

Don shook his head. He suddenly felt rather disorientated. Everything was beginning to feel out of kilter. Now when had it started? Izzy had been her usual slovenly, gloomy self when he had left for the pub. He remembered how fed up he had been; how stale their marriage had seemed. Then there was that strange encounter with "the weirdo", after which he had drunk a fair bit but no more than on a normal Friday night really.

He looked around the room. It was ages since it had been so tidy and clean and much longer since he had enjoyed such a sumptuous breakfast cooked by a glamorous, perfectly groomed wife. He laughed out loud. What was wrong with him? The simple explanation was that Izzy had experienced an epiphany of some sort and decided to change her ways to save their marriage. She couldn't keep the performance up for ever. In fact, he was pretty sure that by the time she returned from the rigours of Saturday morning shopping her bad humour would be thoroughly restored. He would make a joke of it; they would have a laugh and then relax back into the comfort of their usual weekend chaos, but with the benefit of a clean environment and with Izzy looking like a super glamorous version of her usual self. She would be worn out after all her endeavours. She must have done a real impression of Wonder Woman to have achieved all that in a few hours. They would have a nice meal out and all would be well. For now, he was going to take advantage of the situation and catch up on the sports coverage.

Don was contentedly dozing in front of the TV when he heard Izzy's car pull up. He went through to the kitchen to put the kettle on. She'd need a cup of coffee. He expected to hear the usual grunts and groans which would normally have accompanied a solo shopping expedition, but there were none. Indeed, Izzy was smiling and still immaculate as she carried numerous plastic bags into the kitchen and placed them on the counter.

'Oh darling, coffee how lovely,' she exclaimed as

he placed a steaming cup in front of her.

'Izz you can drop the Stepford Wives act now,' he said, laughing.

Izzy merely smiled and reached into one of the bags. 'I've brought back some double choc chip cookies for you, my darling. Let's have one with this delicious coffee.'

'Yeah, yeah,' said Don, 'but honestly love, you can drop the act now. I do appreciate your efforts though. In fact, I'm taking you out tonight. I'm going to book a table at Zackarta's.'

Izzy clapped her hands in glee. 'Wonderful, darling. Now I must put the shopping away and get on with the chores.'

*OK*, thought Don, *if that was the way she wanted to play it. Let her keep up the act for a few hours longer. He'd take her out for an early evening meal at the Italian and once she'd had a few glasses of wine things would be back to normal. God knows what chores she was planning to do though. The house looked absolutely immaculate; as did she. Well, he might as well take advantage of the situation. His team were at home. He'd go down to the ground and catch a Saturday afternoon game for a change. In fact, if anything was going to prompt a sharp response from his wife it would be him "abandoning her at the weekend".*

He sought her out and found her on her hands and knees in the utility room, wearing an apron over her smart casual clothes and turning out a cupboard.

'Thought I'd go off to the match then if you're OK with that?'

Izzy merely turned towards him, smiling. 'That's a lovely idea darling. You enjoy yourself. You work so hard.'

*The woman deserved an Oscar*, he thought. He was glad to get out into the fresh air and join the crowds walking to the game. He had a pint beforehand in the club house. No doubt when he got home Izzy would be back to her normal self, berating him for his muddy boots and beer breath. Anyway, they'd have a good night out tonight and sort things out.

Don just got home in time for a quick shower and change of clothing. He had been amazed when Izzy had greeted him at the door, wearing a lovely blue lace dress he hadn't seen in years. He had no idea she could still get into it.

'Wow,' he said. 'You look beautiful', and she did. It was strange though that she didn't mention the muddy footprints he'd left on the hall floor. He was starting to miss the banter to be honest. She'd merely kissed him on the cheek and thanked him for the compliment.

Zackarta's Italian Restaurant was a short walk from the couple's home, and they arrived in good time. Izzy had told Don how handsome he looked and had held his hand as they walked along making pleasant conversation. They usually had a joke about the staff at the restaurant. It was a family-run business and some of the waiters were a bit temperamental and eccentric. It was part of the fun somehow. However, today Izzy maintained her sunny calm demeanour, greeting Don's remarks and minor criticisms with a squeeze of the hand and saying, 'I'm sure they do their best my darling.' Don suspected it would be a different story in a few hours when the wine had started to flow.

Don had felt very proud of Izzy's appearance. He was sure though it wouldn't be as perfect by the end of the meal. They were both slightly messy eaters and although she loved spaghetti bolognese, Izzy had never quite mastered the art of eating this gracefully. Tonight, however, her technique was faultless, and the beautiful blue dress remained unsplattered. Not so Don's black silk shirt. He looked down at it ruefully, but Izzy merely said. 'Don't worry darling, I'll sponge out those stains when we get home.'

Somehow the evening dragged, even though Don had drunk most of the bottle of Valpolicella single-handedly, Izzy having spurned this after one small glass in favour of water. Don realised he felt desperately lonely. He missed the old Izzy – her quirky acerbic wit, her slightly clumsy ways, the getting rather tipsy together. Who was this strange, exquisite stranger? She looked and sounded like the perfect wife, but she wasn't actually perfect for him.

As they walked home, Izzy thanked Don for a wonderful evening. Normally, at this point, she would have been complaining about her smart shoes and would probably have flung them off, and Don would have carried them. They would have laughed and joked about the meal; but tonight she walked sedately beside him, just remarking on the pleasant evening.

He was pleased when they arrived home. The alcohol was beginning to wear off and he felt a bit strange and uncomfortable. Izzy hung up their coats and told him to go and sit down whilst she made them a coffee, but he couldn't settle and suddenly he knew what he must do and before midnight.

The Tipsy Toad was just as busy as the previous evening. They even had bouncers on the door to cope with the Saturday night revellers. Don forced his way through the throng. All the tables were packed, and they were standing three deep at the bar. He searched wildly round the room. A group of rowdy girls were sitting at the table he and Wilbur had occupied the previous night – probably a hen party. He envied their carefree drunken abandon. It was almost eleven. It was madness but it seemed his one chance, otherwise he could not imagine the horrible "perfect" future that he would be forced to endure.

Then at last he saw a figure squashed up on a stool close to the bar wearing a strange, crooked felt hat. Don ran over to Wilbur and gripped his arm. 'Please,' he begged, 'let me have your last spell.'

Don cautiously pushed open the front door. The house was quiet, almost, apart from the sound of snoring coming from the lounge. Izzy lay on the settee with her mouth open, her eye makeup smeared across her face. He leant over her and stroked her messy fringe away from her forehead. She opened one eye. 'What you doing, you daft bugger?' she asked.

'I love you Izzy,' Don said, kissing her lovely soft familiar face.

# THE RIGHT CHOICE

'It's alright for you,' Tyro said.' You've always known, haven't you?'

'I suppose so.' Esto curled a lock of hair around their finger.' I've always imagined wearing blue silk, dainty shoes, make-up and jewellery.'

'It must be nice to be so certain. Yeah, you know I can see you in all that silk shit and . . . ,' Tyro peered at Esto's eyes, 'you've got the right eyelashes – yeah, I reckon you're going to be a real, what did they used to call it? *Femme fatale*.'

'Mmm, don't know about that but one of my first memories is seeing an ancient book, must have belonged to one of the oldies. Anyway, in it was this story about a princess who had a ballgown made of that really blue sky you get on a sunny day. Sounds weird, huh, but that's the sort of dress I've always imagined having. Bit of a change to this.' Esto prodded the leg of their neutro-suit. 'Doesn't come in sky-blue, does it? Oh, but I'm rocking such a brilliant shade of pale khaki today.'

Tyro laughed, 'You know what? I kinda prefer the mid-grey. Goes well with my eyes, don't you think?' Tyro opened their eyes wide.' Although I think Mumpy prefers me in the taupe.'

'Tyro, do you still call your mother-parent that?'

'Yes, and father-parent will always be Dadster to me. I suppose now you're almost gender-ready you've moved on to MP and FP?'

'Well, yes, but Tyro just be serious for a minute. Have you really no idea?' Esto moved over to the mirror, concentrating on their reflection. 'You've got to make your mind up, you know. You'll be seventeen soon. Unless you want to stay gender neutral.' Esto paused, frowning as they considered this possibility. 'Anyway,' they continued, 'I'm going to be starting treatment the week after next. First off, it's just the capsules, then you get some counselling before the laser stuff. I'm not looking forward to that, but they say it's practically painless, and I should be completely gender-defined by the end of year prom. I'm going to adopt a feminine version of my given name. I'm going to be Estelle.'

'Yeah, so you might get your sky-blue dream after all.' Tyro squinted at Esto trying to imagine their friend as a shapely female in a glamorous gown. Actually, it wasn't that difficult. Tyro thought there was something soft and feminine about Esto despite the shapeless boiler suits which came in three neutral shades and were required wear for children and young people until their gender assignment was complete.

'Well, I think I may have to save up for a while for that, but I'll get there eventually, I guess.' For a moment Esto looked sad.

Tyro felt a bit awkward. They'd forgotten that

Esto's family weren't well off but remembered now Mumpy saying something about Esto's father-parent having had a disagreement with one of the Guardians which had led to the family's status being downgraded.

'I've got to get off.' Tyro was suddenly keen to be outside, alone and preferably walking briskly or even running.

* * *

Tyro's mother-parent was in the living area, sorting through some paperwork. She looked up as Tyro entered.

'Oh good, you've just arrived at the right time. Guardian Sullivan has been pestering me about your Intention Papers.'

'Mumpy, I've got some stuff I've got to sort.' Tyro turned to walk up the stairs.

'Tyro, you've been putting this off for weeks and we just can't anymore. Let's go through the paperwork together. Guardian Sullivan says it helps to define your choices.'

Tyro slouched back into the living area and squatted down beside Mumpy. 'I don't know why you still call it paperwork – there's been no paper involved since, well forever.'

'Don't be so pedantic.' She pulled out the AdminPad and spoke into it, '13 April 2089, 1300 hours, Intention Papers in respect of Tyro Darlington.'

'Subject's thumbprint and retinal recognition

required for this transaction,' was the automated response.

Tyro winced. He wished Mumpy would upgrade so they had a choice of voices. If their friends knew they were still using Auto Annie, they'd have a spasm.

'So come on Tyro.' Mumpy hauled them over and thrust their thumb onto the sensor, twisting their head so a retinal response could be obtained in the MagiEye. 'Let's get on with it. You know me and Dadster will have a fine to pay if we don't complete the IPs soon.'

Tyro flopped onto the relaxster. They knew when they were beaten.

'So, first question, do you believe you have been provided with sufficient information with regard to gender allocation?'

'Yeah, suppose so,' muttered Tyro.

'Have you a natural inclination towards female or male assignment?'

'No, dunno, Mumpy do we really have to do this now?' Tyro slunk further down into the relaxster.

'Tyro, do you really want to end up a gender neutral? I don't know. Your great-grandparents would have killed to have been given this opportunity. Do you realise what a privilege it is to be able to choose a gender? Do you realise how hard your ancestors had to fight to give you this freedom of choice? Can you imagine what it was like in the olden days when people were born in the wrong bodies?'

'Yeah, Mumpy you've told me all this before.'

'But I don't think you realise just how much suffering people endured. They faced ridicule, mental torment and incredibly painful surgical procedures, and sometimes they lived their whole lives as the wrong gender. How lucky we are to be in true control of our own destinies.'

'Well, I just need a little bit longer to think. I'm sorry Mumpy, but there it is.'

Mumpy saw a tear sliding down Tyro's cheek and softened. Perhaps this was a good sign. She knew it was an official misdemeanour to influence your child's choice of gender in any way, but she only had one child and desperately wanted a girl. She hadn't been hopeful that this would be Tyro's chosen path but maybe they were embracing their more feminine, sensitive side. She decided on a different approach.

'OK, Tyro. I don't want you upset. Let's leave it for a couple of days. There is something you may enjoy doing though. You know that myself and Dadster plan to give you a gender allocation gift.'

'Yeah. Thanks.' Tyro wiped the sleeve of their neutro-suit across their face.

'So, we've put some credit into EUNAD and come up with a list for you to choose from. Take some time now to have a look through and beam your choice down so I can get it ordered.'

Tyro went up to their room and accessed EUNAD (it was an acronym for Everything You Need And Desire, and an easy way to order absolutely anything and have it robotically transferred to your home). They saw that Mumpy and Dadster had been very generous with their selections.

There was a motorised transporter, handy for getting around and easy to fold away; a top of the range sensory system incorporating every sort of sound and vision experience you could imagine; and a Dream Machine which allowed you to record your dream brainwaves and replay the ones you most enjoyed. There were also less adventurous but highly desirable items such as some wildly expensive designer clothing. Tyro knew this was the one occasion when they would be allowed an extravagant gift as it marked the most important decision they would ever make. Eventually, Tyro made a choice and beamed the details down to Mumpy.

Mumpy breathed a sigh of pure contentment when she saw what Tyro had chosen. There were times when she hadn't been hopeful but now it seemed that all her dreams were about to come true.

\* \* \*

The next day Tyro bounded down the stairs, a big box in their hands. Mumpy had heard a gasp of delight from upstairs and guessed that Tyro had found the gift which had been delivered whilst they were at The Learning Hub. But as Tyro entered the living area, Mumpy stepped back in surprise. Tyro was wearing a neutro-suit accessorised with some sort of camouflage baseball cap and black boots.

'Thanks Mumpy.' Tyro blew their mother a kiss and waved the box in the air. 'This is brilliant. I love you. Just off out. We'll do those IPs when I get back.'

Tyro was out of the door before Mumpy had time to respond. She sank down on the relaxster, completely perplexed.

* * *

'This is for you,' said Tyro handing the box to Esto. 'I want you to wear it when you accompany me to the end of year prom. I hope that you'll deem me a suitable partner.'

Esto opened the box and pulled out a beautiful sky-blue silk dress. 'So, Tyro, I guess you've made your choice.'

'Tyrone at your service my beautiful Estelle and, yes, now you can address me as "he".'

# A PRECIOUS GIFT

Derek sealed the cream envelope and popped it into the box. He closed the lid and admired his handiwork. The construction of the jewellery box had given him great pleasure. He imagined Jane opening his present on Christmas Day, running her fingers over the beautiful mahogany veneer and looking with delight at the pattern of entwined leaves which decorated the lid, surrounding the letter "J" which he had carved with great care.

He knew Jane didn't possess a lot of jewellery – just a signet ring which her parents had bought her for her 18th birthday and a locket which he had presented to her on her 20th. He had been so pleased and proud when she insisted that he provide a small photograph of himself so that she could place it inside.  Up until then he could not imagine that anyone would want a photo of him. He wasn't handsome and strong like his brother, Henry. He was a bit nondescript-looking really with pale freckled skin and thin, sandy-coloured hair. His mother said he had nice eyes, well, "kind eyes" she said and good hands. He had to admit that he was proud of his hands. His fingers were long and slender, and he loved making things, small, decorative items out of wood. He was in a world of his own when absorbed with one of his marquetry projects; a world in which he had control and could construct beautiful objects. His father and brother thought this pastime was a bit effeminate.

'Could understand it if you made summat useful, our Derek,' Henry had said. 'Mam could do with a couple of solid kitchen chairs.'

Derek thought that in that case Henry should have a go at making them instead of going down the pub as soon as he came in from the pit, but he didn't say so. Henry had a quick temper and was handy with his fists. He took after his dad he supposed. But he knew it couldn't be easy working down the pit. He had dreaded the thought of it. He had worked hard at school and got taken on as a clerk in a local firm of auctioneers. He had thought himself very lucky but then the Germans refused to remove troops from Belgium and King George declared war on Germany.

First off the army put out a call for volunteers and half a million men enlisted in the first couple of months but as the war raged on it became obvious that there were too few volunteers to fill the ranks and at the beginning of 1916 The Military Service Bill introduced conscription for all eligible single men between 18 and 41. Henry said he would have been happy to go and sort out the Huns but his was a reserved occupation. Derek's mother thought that he might fail the medical as he was slightly built and didn't have the strong constitution of his elder sibling, but he was passed as physically fit and no exemption was provided for an auctioneer's clerk.

Derek was filled with dread at the prospect. Strangely, it wasn't fighting the enemy that scared him the most. It was the thought of living cheek by jowl with numerous other recruits; of having no privacy. He imagined countless scenarios in which he was ridiculed or abused by his fellow soldiers. His experience at school had not been happy and physically and mentally he had been ill-equipped to cope with bullies and those who sneered at his sensitivities. He imagined that life in the army would offer up a similar experience. He prayed every night that by some miracle the war would end before his basic training began.

Focussing on his gift for Jane had been a blessed escape from the reality that faced him. Jane had been heart-broken when she had realised that he would be away at Christmas. Derek told her that he would be leaving a special gift with her that she should open on Christmas morning. He hoped that it would be a nice surprise and that her response to the letter inside would be favourable. The thick cream envelope simply bore Jane's name. The letter inside read:

*My Dearest Jane,*

*It is so hard to be away from you at this time. Do you remember last Christmas, my darling? We had only just met but I was so delighted that you agreed to meet my family on Boxing Day. I was very proud of you. You looked beautiful in your blue dress and I knew right away that I wanted to spend every Christmas with you by my side.*

*Well this Christmas we can't be together, but I want you to know that I will be thinking of you constantly and imagining you opening my gift to you. If I had the money this box would contain a very special piece of jewellery, an engagement ring because I'm asking you, dearest Jane, if you will do me the very great honour of becoming my wife?*

*I love you so much my darling and I promise that if you agree to be my wife, I will do my best to give you the happy life that you deserve.*

*With all my love,*

*Derek*

Derek wondered whether he would have had the courage to propose to Jane if they had been spending Christmas together. He could not imagine what she saw in him but was constantly thrilled when her small hand enclosed his and held it so tightly. She made him feel that he was tall and powerful. He wanted to protect her and care for her always. They spent the day together before he left for basic training. It was very special indeed. The memory was to sustain Derek for many months to come.

Jane had kept her promise to Derek and opened his gift on Christmas Day. She had marvelled at the beauty of the jewellery box and was delighted to discover the envelope inside. She had clung to the letter and cried when she had read his proposal. It was truly wonderful to her that he felt the same as she did. She was confident now that he would welcome her news; the news that would change both their lives and mean that they would become a real family. She composed a response straight away.

* * *

Derek's mother was sitting in Jane's mother's parlour when Jane got back from work. She looked old and drawn. Jane knew right away that it was bad. She went over to her and put a hand on her shoulder.

'Mrs Taskins, it's not good is it?' she asked.

'No, love, the worst, I'm afraid. But Janie, he died a hero. He was helping some wounded chap, a private Cyril Chapman apparently. They say he might have saved himself if he hadn't stopped to help. Anyway, this Cyril survived because of him.'

Molly Taskins was overcome with grief for a minute but then managed to compose herself. She opened her handbag and drew out a small package of letters.

'These are what you wrote to him, lovie. He would have wanted you to have them and they also found this. Looks like he had written a letter to you just before ...' She broke down again but handed Jane the letters. Then she looked at Jane properly for the first time and noticed how tightly her winter coat strained across her stomach.

'Oh, Janie, Janie,' she said, grasping the young girl's hand.

As soon as she was alone, Jane tore open the letter from Derek.

*My darling, darling Jane,*

*You have made me the happiest man alive and I can face anything today because of you. My heart is swelling with joy and the news you have given me is so wonderful.*

*It won't be too long before I'm due some leave and we can marry but in my heart you are already my wife and it is so wonderful that our union has already been blessed.*

*Please don't worry too much about me. Conditions may be very primitive, but I have made some good friends with like-minded folk here such as Cyril, who has also had some very good news today. He has just become a father and hopes to get leave in the next week or so.*

*I love you so much Jane. You have made me strong, please stay strong for us,*

*Derek*

It was of great comfort to know that at least Derek had received her letter and had died in a happy state of mind *and* bravely saving the life of his friend. Jane vowed that she *would* do her best to stay strong.

\* \* \*

25<sup>th</sup> December 1917 and Jane sat in the cottage that she shared with her family. They were at the Christmas morning service, but she had chosen to stay behind, sitting by the fire in the parlour. However, she was not alone, she cuddled baby John Derek on her knee as she read to him the last letter from his father.

Reluctantly, she put the letter back in its envelope and placed it with the others in her jewellery box. She ran her finger over the lid, marvelling at the intricacy of the craftsmanship. She loved the box; it provided a tangible expression of Derek's love for her.

'One day you'll make your father proud,' she whispered to her son, 'because you're going to be a fine man, just like him.'

# TRUST ME

I wouldn't say I actually looked forward to work but, compared to some jobs I'd had, working in Hendersons' warehouse was OK. In that sort of place, it all depends on your workmates to lighten the load and offset the tedium. Daz, Billy, Mungo, Pete and me were a pretty good team. I'd been there coming up for five years and a couple of years previously had been made up to supervisor. Didn't make a lot of difference really, a few quid extra in my pay packet and a bit more responsibility sometimes. Like when our line manager Jason was off, which he had been the day I first met Brian. He'd had to go down to Blackpool on some sort of managers' jaunt.

Before he left he'd said, 'Eddie, I'm gonna have to leave you to it. You know what we're looking for. A hard worker and someone who can fit right in with you and the rest of the lads. It's just a temporary vacancy anyway at the moment.'

So, there I was, Senior Warehouse Operative, sitting behind Jason's desk and making decisions on recruitment. I had a bit of help from HR. They'd sent Sally over to make sure I didn't do or say anything politically incorrect but, basically, I had the final say.

Jason had whittled the applicants down to three

because he'd said that it was daft spending all day interviewing for someone who was just gonna be helping out over Christmas. There was a standard proforma to work to and Sally said she would help me score the interviewees' responses. I'd put a shirt and tie on under my overall. Tanya had insisted on ironing it. I'd told her not to bother too much because basically only the collar and a bit at the front would be showing but it looked more professional than wearing my usual Led Zeppelin tee-shirt.

The first guy neither me nor Sally took to. He was arrogant and it was obvious he thought the job beneath him. He didn't answer my questions very well, so his scores were rubbish and me and Sally both gave him the thumbs down as soon as he'd left the office.

The next one was very young and earnest. He'd got a bit of relevant experience working for one of our competitors, and he seemed to know what we were looking for but, you know what, I couldn't take to him somehow. I thought he was too quiet. Couldn't really see him fitting in with the rest of the lads. Sally was obviously very impressed though.

She'd been completing her scoring matrix and said to me, 'Eddie, unless the next candidate is brilliant, I think we've found our temporary warehouse operative.'

I'd just looked at her. 'Sally, trust me, he's too quiet. The lads are gonna make mincemeat out of him.'

Anyway, we were down to the last bloke and when Brian walked in, I took to him right away. He looked like he knew his way around, and he had a cheeky grin. Sally was frowning though as she filled in her matrix. She didn't seem as enthusiastic as I was. After he'd left she shook her head.

'Nice guy, Eddie, but not really enough specific experience and I'm not confident he grasps what a dangerous place a warehouse can be. We'd be better with the second candidate. He's worked in a similar role and would take the job seriously.'

'Yeah, Sally,' I'd said. 'Way too seriously. I reckon he verged on the neurotic if you want to know. Trust me. I know people. Brian's our man. He'll get on well with the lads and pick up the job quickly.'

Sally had sighed but had agreed that I had the final say. I could see she wasn't happy though. Well tough. I was sure Brian was our man. He'd soon learn the ropes and be up for a bit of a laugh I'd thought.

Anyway, when I rang Brian to give him the good news he was over the moon. Said he thought he hadn't stood a chance because in his words 'that bird didn't seem to take to me.' Said he was really chuffed to have landed the job if the rest of the crew were like me.

I was right about the lads taking to Brian. He was easy-going and appreciative of any help given to him. We had to give him a heads up on a few bits and pieces because he'd not actually worked in a warehouse before; but no-one minded. You couldn't help but like him. His jokes were entertaining. A bit near the knuckle sometimes but he was savvy enough to keep his mouth shut when management were around. At the end of the first week, he hung around after the others had gone whilst I was filling in the timesheets. Said he wanted to treat me to a pint to say thank you for all the help I'd given him. I was keen to get home really but he had this engaging way about him. Said I'd just join him for one. Well, we got on like a house on fire. We made it a regular thing after that. He had this wicked sense of humour and was a great mimic. Took off management, especially Jason, to a "T". It was nice to have a drinking buddy and let off a bit of steam together.

I think Tanya began to feel a bit left out. I suggested to Brian that he and his missus and me and Tanya should have a night out together, but he said his wife didn't go out much. Apparently, she wasn't in the best of health. Then he'd shut up. It was obvious he didn't want to talk about her. Tanya thought it was a bit strange. She kept asking questions, but I wasn't about to interrogate the guy.

Anyway, he was getting a bit edgy because he was coming up to the end of his contract and, to be honest, I didn't think he'd be kept on after Christmas as things tended to quieten down a bit in January. Trouble was he'd had to take some time off as well due to taking his missus to hospital appointments. I didn't know the details about what was wrong with her and wasn't about to ask but on the quiet I managed to fix it so he'd been able to slip off early a few times. Thought I had it covered but Brian told me that Billy had noticed and not been too happy about it. He said he didn't want to tell me. He'd looked really embarrassed about it, but I insisted he tell me all. Then he said Billy had been giving him a hard time about not having as much experience as the rest of them, and also been bad-mouthing me to some extent, saying I shouldn't have taken him on. That I didn't have experience to handle recruitment and was getting way above myself. Brian said he felt a right Judas. But I was glad he'd told me. I was really disappointed in Billy. Thought I would have to watch him from then on as I only wanted lads around me I could trust. Thought I would have to wait and see what the New Year brought.

Anyway, come January and Brian was still around as there was a vacancy when Billy got the push. Apparently, he'd been thieving. Jason got a tip-off to search his locker and three boxes of Bluetooth headsets were found. Acted like he was amazed, but he'd been seen putting them in. Jason wouldn't say by who. Anyway, after what Brian had said I wasn't surprised. Looked as though he was a nasty piece of work, trying to make trouble behind my back.

Brian's face was a picture when he got a

permanent contract. He said it was just the bit of good news his missus needed. I asked how she was doing. Said me and Tanya would love for them both to come round for a meal but he got embarrassed, said that would be wonderful if she carried on improving but just at the moment she couldn't face anyone. I really felt for him and completely understood his need to be late into work and sometimes having to slip off early. Course I covered for him. I explained to Tanya that sometimes I had to stay on a bit in the evenings. There were a couple of occasions when he'd put the stock in the wrong section. I started to do a few last-minute checks before I left. His mind obviously wasn't on the job. Too much on his mind. I would have been in pieces if it had been Tanya.

Then in March Jason and Mr Blackfriars called me in. They said that the warehouse wasn't meeting some of its targets and that they were gonna have to monitor things closely over the next few months. Mr Blackfriars said it was, in his words, 'time I stepped up to the plate and got my team back on track.' Jason came to find me afterwards – asked me if everything was all right at home. Said I didn't seem my usual happy self. Well, I was tired. The hours were long enough before but now I was in earlier and staying behind trying to cover for Brian. I didn't begrudge it. Cos I thought he'd do the same for me. Tanya was a bit fed up though. Said I was putting work before her. She thought I should confide in Jason. Tell him about Brian's situation. I told her she didn't understand.

Brian's situation seemed to be getting worse. He said if it wasn't for me he'd go mad with worry. I was the best mate he'd ever had, and he'd always be in my debt. He said he knew I wouldn't grass him up to the management because he said that Jason was two-faced and always made sure he had an easy time of it. He said that no-one worked as hard as me in the company but people like Jason would take credit for the work that I did. I began to think there might be something in that. Jason had always seemed OK to me, but I started thinking that perhaps he'd been taking advantage of my good nature. Brian thought I ought to stand up for myself a bit more. Maybe let Jason know that I'd sussed him.

I told Tanya what Brian had said. She looked at me a bit funny and said, 'Eddie just be careful.' I thought she might have a soft spot for Jason. When she'd met him at a works social she'd said he was "a nice young man".

I thought that Brian was a man of the world and that he knew what was what. He said maybe I shouldn't always be so amenable when Jason asked me to do something.

Then a couple of months later Brian's missus seemed to be making a recovery and his work improved. In fact, he got a special mention at the staff meeting for suggesting some improvements to the stacking system. I was glad Jason was impressed. I seemed to remember coming up with the idea a few months earlier and talking to Brian about it down the pub. I didn't think he remembered. I knew how your memory can play tricks on you especially when you've had a few drinks. When I mentioned it to him after the staff meeting he obviously felt bad.

'Ah mate,' he'd said, striking his forehead, 'yes, I do remember we talked through something like that  and it did set me off on the right lines. Perhaps I should have given you some credit. Oh man, I'm sorry. With everything that's been going on, I just didn't think.'

I didn't know what to think but all that I believed was that not for one minute would he have taken all the credit intentionally. Mainly I was so chuffed that things were going better for him.

Then a week or so later Jason started in on those performance targets again. For once I stood up for myself and told him I was working really hard, and perhaps he could give me a bit more support. He looked surprised. I thought perhaps he would start to have a bit more respect for me. But I felt uncomfortable somehow. It wasn't like me to get into a confrontation situation with management.

Brian saw me looking worried. When I told him what Jason had said, he said it was funny that Jason and Mr Blackfriars still had time to skive off to play golf.

'Maybe that's where you're going wrong, Eddie,'

he'd suggested. 'Maybe you need to do a bit of networking; get yourself a set of clubs, mate.'

I'd laughed but, you know what, I started thinking he might have hit the nail on the head. One rule for the management and another for the rest of us. I had my performance review coming up though and just hoped my bonus wasn't in jeopardy.

Normally the reviews were a pretty laid-back affair, but they started in on me straight away. Said warehouse performance was way down. What was I going to do about it? I'd looked from Jason to old Blackfrairs. I couldn't believe the tone they were taking.

'I put in a lot of unpaid overtime to keep the show on the road,' I'd told them. 'Not all of us spend half our lives on the golf course.'

Things went from bad to worse after that. Next thing I knew I was calling Jason all the names under the sun and old Blackfriars said there was no way I could continue in my present role in view of my insubordination. Insubordination? I told them what they could do with the job and stormed out.

I went and got the stuff out of my locker and saw a couple of the lads and told them I was off. I was so angry I couldn't tell them what had kicked off. Daz tried to get me to calm down, but I wasn't having any of it. Brian wasn't around. He'd booked half a day's leave. When I got home, I sent him a text. I thought he would be upset and angry on my behalf. I didn't want him to walk into a bad scene the next day. I thought he would probably ring me straight away when he got the news, but he didn't, but I thought maybe he had gone somewhere without his phone.

Then I got drunk as the proverbial skunk. Tanya said she couldn't believe what had happened as I'd been so happy with the lads at Hendersons. She was on at me the next morning before she went to work. Said she thought I ought to make an appointment to see Jason and go in and eat humble pie. She asked me what Brian had said. I realised then that I hadn't heard from him. Checked my phone to make sure I had sent him that text. I had but I thought mobiles can be funny sometimes. Sent him another. I didn't want him to walk into work unprepared. Eventually, around mid-morning, he'd replied. I wondered if he'd not properly understood the situation because all his text said was: *So sorry mate. Speak soon.*

I was in a right state all day. I thought that Brian must be devastated and hoped he didn't put his job in jeopardy sticking up for me. I tried to ring him a few times, but his phone always just went to voicemail. I thought that maybe he was in shock. Finally, around eight o'clock at night I got a message saying: *Things a bit hectic at moment mate. Catch up with you later.* I started to have some weird thoughts then but couldn't believe Brian would let me down.

I had a very bad few days but the following week I got my act together and went into town, down the Job Centre and looking up a few contacts. Bumped into Billy of all people. He said he'd heard I'd got the push at Hendersons. Apparently he was still in touch with old Daz. Said the lads weren't liking the situation one bit. Brian wasn't half the supervisor I'd been. I couldn't make sense of it. Billy had laughed but not in a nasty way. Think he felt sorry for me.

'Look mate,' he'd said, 'he played you for a right fool, but Daz said they could see it coming, specially when he started to hang round Jason. Now the two of them are as thick as thieves which, by the way, I never was, and you don't need to be a genius to figure out who set me up. Mind you that Jason wants to watch his back cos Brian'll be having his job next.'

Eighteen months on and that is exactly what happened. Saw Brian last week at The Precinct getting out of a fancy BMW. He didn't see me, nose in the air striding off with his phone pressed against his ear. Looked pretty stressed actually. But me, every day's like playtime now. Couldn't get a job immediately when I got the push from Hendersons, but the Job Centre got me on this scheme as a trainee mechanic. Always loved tinkering with engines. When I qualify, I'm gonna set up my own business and Tanya's gonna do the books. Sometimes things do work out for the best. Trust me.

# THE LANGUAGE OF LOVE

Hetty was bored. Her mother had told her that only boring people were bored and that there were a thousand and one ways she could usefully occupy herself. Therein lay the problem. Useful occupation held no attraction for Hetty. What she craved was frivolous distraction, but this generally proved costly and Mr and Mrs Jessop, whilst able to provide a moderately comfortable lifestyle, had, as Mr Jessop often admonished his daughter, 'nought left over for frills and fancies.'

That afternoon Hetty had the house to herself, apart from the Jessops' maid of all work, Sarah, and her daughter, Mary, who had recently joined her mother to assist with household chores. Aged just eighteen, she was the same age as Hetty, and the two girls had known each other all their lives. Privately, Mary thought Hetty very spoiled and privileged. In common with many young girls in the early nineteenth century, Mary had received very little schooling and been in service since her early teens. Her previous employment had been in a much grander establishment where she had worked her way up from kitchen maid to parlour maid, but she had lost that post she said because 'the missus was allus jealous of me.' However, Mrs Jessop had decided that she would not delve too deeply into that. It worked to her advantage that Mary was urgently in need of a new post and willing to accept very modest wages. She reasoned that the girl's mother would mostly be around to "keep the lass in hand" and so far the arrangement was working very well.

There was a relaxed atmosphere as Mr and Mrs Jessop were visiting relatives and were not due back for an evening meal. So Sarah had made herself comfortable, sitting in the kitchen with her feet up tackling a pile of darning. Mary had been tasked with cleaning the silver in the parlour and she and Hetty were taking the opportunity to have a good gossip which would have been frowned on had Mrs Jessop been at home.

'Mary, I'm so bored,' moaned Hetty. 'Nothing happens around here.' She put down the sampler she was supposed to be embroidering and walked over to where Mary was polishing.

'Wish I'd got the time to be bored,' sniffed Mary. Chance would be a fine thing.' She pushed back a blonde curl inside her cap. 'I hate wearing this thing,' she complained. 'I look a right sight in it. At least the one at Lady Fanshaw's had lace round it.'

Impetuously, she pulled the cap off and swung her head so that her luxuriant hair fell around her shoulders.

Hetty looked at her enviously. 'Likely, you'll be married soon enough, with a brood of children and a fine handsome husband to take care of.'

'Yes,' agreed Mary, 'but what I wouldn't give to

be able to sit around all afternoon in a fine gown waiting for the maid to bring my afternoon tea.'

She gave a mischievous curtsey and laughed. Hetty laughed along with her. The two of them could talk like this when no-one was around. She had to agree though that Mary would have looked lovely in a smart dress, especially the blue silk one she was wearing which was trimmed with lace and had little pearl buttons. It was her second-best dress and her mother had told her to wear it because Aunt Jemima was visiting in the area and had said that she would call round that afternoon. She hadn't seen young Hetty since she was a little girl and so it was agreed that it would be pleasant for the two to get reacquainted. Hetty had been given a list of instructions by her mother. She must be polite and pleasant and ensure that her aunt was provided with light refreshments. Hetty was not thrilled with the prospect. She remembered Aunt Jemima as a thin dour woman who had patted her on the head and told her that 'little girls should be seen and not heard.' She had a couple of hours to herself before the visit and was desperate for some diversion. Then suddenly an amusing thought occurred to her.

'Well, I think we should change places, just for the afternoon.'

Mary looked confused but without further ado Hetty took her hand and led her upstairs where she persuaded her to try on the blue silk. It did look lovely. Mary twirled around happily. Hetty put on Mary's discarded uniform. She was suddenly energised and purposeful. She sat Mary at the dressing table and proceeded to style her hair.

Mary started to look a bit worried. 'Hetty, don't you think we'd better change back. Your visitor 'll be 'ere soon and I've got that silver to finish.'

'Never mind that,' scolded Hetty. 'Now sit still whilst I put this clip in your hair. I'm going to put a little of this rouge on you as well. Now what a fine lady you look.'

To complete the transformation, Hetty changed Mary's brown working boots for fine satin slippers and covered her work-worn hands with a pair of lacy gloves. She stood back to admire the results. Then she realised that there was one unresolved issue.

'Just one thing, your voice. Now what can we do about that?' Hetty thought for a moment, then was hit with an inspiration. 'I know, you've lost your voice. You've had a chill and lost your voice, and the doctor has advised you not to try to strain it. So, have you got that Mary, no talking whatsoever?' She tapped Mary sharply on the shoulder.

Mary looked a little alarmed but then she caught sight of her reflection in the mirror. She did look rather splendid in the blue silk. The dress fitted her perfectly. On Hetty it had begun to strain slightly on the bodice and under the arms. Her inactive lifestyle meant that she was beginning to gain a few rather unbecoming surplus pounds

'Just be careful with that dress,' warned Hetty. Now come on. Let's get you settled before Aunt Jemima arrives. I need to let her in. We don't want your mother coming up from the kitchen; but not much chance of that I'm guessing. She'll be taking the chance of a snooze by the fire whilst my parents are away.'

The two had no sooner got Mary settled in the parlour when there was a knock at the front door. Hetty scurried to answer it. She thought that it was a good thing that she possessed excellent acting skills. As she walked to the door, she practised a downcast look and prepared herself to adopt what she assumed to be an authentic accent.

'Yes Ma'am,' she muttered, as, half curtseying, she opened the door to Aunt Jemima and, surprisingly, a young man. She daren't look at him too directly but could see that he was actually quite handsome with thick dark brown hair and a slim athletic build; he was dressed fashionably in a dark green jacket and brown breeches. In contrast, Aunt Jemima looked rather dowdy in a dark grey walking costume, her thin greying hair pulled back into a tight bun.

'Mrs Jemima Saddleworth calling on Miss Hetty Jessop,' stated the fine lady imperiously. 'And, oh yes, accompanied by Mr Jeremy Watters. Please hurry along and tell her we are here. We are on a tight schedule today.'

'Yes, Ma'am,' mumbled Hetty, just in time remembering to add, 'and begging your pardon,

Ma'am, but the young miss has quite lost her voice. I've to tell you so she don't put a strain on it like.'

Aunt Jemima glared at her. Hetty hurried away back to the parlour where she warned Mary that there was an extra visitor. 'Just smile and nod,' she emphasised. 'I don't think they'll stay long.'

Hetty showed the visitors into the parlour and went off to organise light refreshments. As she went down the stairs to the kitchen, she could hear Sarah snoring loudly. From that point of view, they were safe.

After embracing Mary in a slightly awkward hug, Aunt Jemima introduced the young man. 'Now this young gentleman is my godson, Mr Jeremy Watters. It is such a shame that you have no voice today because he is recently returned from France, and I had thought that you two could have such a lovely conversation. Your mother tells me that you are very skilled in the French language. Never mind. He can talk and you can listen.' She patted Mary's hand reassuringly.

Mary smiled prettily and it seemed that was all she needed to do. She had no idea what Jeremy Watters was talking about. She just kept nodding and smiling. Aunt Jemima gazed proudly at her godson.

When Hetty entered the room with the tea tray she was surprised to hear some of the things Jeremy was saying. She looked in alarm at Mary, but she seemed to be taking it in her stride. She gathered that Aunt Jemima's knowledge of French

SKIN DEEP

must also be somewhat limited. Otherwise, she doubted that Jeremy Watters would be offering such extravagant compliments which appeared to be progressing to rather salacious suggestions. Surely, she thought, he must wonder why the lady to whom he was addressing them did not appear surprised or offended.

Eventually, though, Aunt Jemima tired of being excluded from the conversation and insisted that her godson revert to English. In either language he certainly liked the sound of his own voice as he boastfully told of his exploits on the continent during his Grand Tour. Hetty thought that Mary was beginning to look a little strained. She wondered if she could do anything to expedite the visitors' departure, but Aunt Jemima noticed that she was still in the room and shooed her out saying. 'Off you go, girl. We will ring when we are ready to leave.'

As Hetty left the room, she heard Jeremy saying to Mary, 'Cette fille. Stupide aussi bien que simple.'

It took all her self-control not to make a sharp retort. Well, she may look plain compared to Mary, especially disguised as she was as a maid, but she was certainly not stupid. He was the stupid one, being taken in so easily by a pretty face. She sat down on the stairs straining to hear what they were saying but the parlour door was too thick. Eventually she heard the bell ring and went into the room to show them out. Mary was rather red in the face.

'Such a shame we have to leave so soon,' simpered Aunt Jemima, 'but somehow I don't think it will be the last you will see of this young man.' She tapped Jeremy on the shoulder.

Jeremy took Mary's hand and held it to his lips. Hetty was horrified when she heard him say, 'Cher Hetty, Je ne peux pass attendre que tu sois ma femme.' And further horrified when Mary smiled and nodded her head.

After hastily seeing the visitors out, Hetty returned to the parlour to find Mary stuffing leftover cakes into her mouth.

'What a relief that's over,' she said, laughing.

'Mmm,' said Hetty. 'I think you may have just accepted his marriage proposal.'

Neither of them knew whether to laugh or cry, but at least Hetty was no longer bored.

# THE AWFUL TRUTH

'What's the deal with you and Julia?' asked Nathan. 'You always seem so tense when you talk about her.'

Sarah picked up her bottle of beer and took a long slug. She looked out of the small window. The view was not very inspiring. She had to stand on a chair to get a glimpse of any green space between the three-storey semis and terraced properties, many of which had been converted into flats and bedsits. But the dreary Manchester suburb had convenient transport links to the city and at least now she had her own small shower room and kitchenette. She sighed. Nathan moved over to stand behind her, linking his arms around her waist and kissing the top of her head, smoothing down his hands over her long blonde hair.

'Tell me about it when you feel ready,' he said.

She and Nathan had only been a couple for a few months, but they spent most of their free time together and he was very sensitive to her feelings. It was one of the things she loved about him. She turned to give him a hug and ruffled his light brown hair, which she loved, it reminded her of a teddy bear, as did his soft hazel eyes which glowed with intelligence and mischief.

She thought she should confide in him but

her relationship with her sister was difficult and complex. Some elements were painful to recall, and generally she avoided thinking or talking about Julia. Nathan was one of six, a middle child in a noisy, happy family. There was nothing complex about his relationship with his siblings. Sometimes they irritated and annoyed him, but mostly he loved them unconditionally. However, now Julia had announced her intention to visit the following day to impart some "big news". So, for the first time, Julia and Nathan would meet.

'Well, we've never been close really Nath. We're just quite different, and there's a fairly large age gap between us.'

Nathan looked unconvinced by this explanation. 'Well, I'm looking forward to meeting her. I've not met any of your family so far. I was beginning to think you might be ashamed of me.'

'You know how I feel about you, and you'll be seeing Mum and Dad soon, but I don't see them all that much. They're busy people and with them living a fair distance away we only meet up a few times a year. Julia sees Mum more often because they've always been really close. They're very alike except Mum's a lot nicer.'

'Hey Sarah, you really don't like that sister of yours, do you?'

'It's not that Nath. It's just, well, I find it hard to trust her.'

Nathan looked appalled. Sarah thought she had better tell him the full story.

*   *   *

Sarah remembered the day that Julia had decided to tell her "the awful truth". Sarah had been sitting on Nanna Pat's knee having her hair braided into a French plait. Julia had been doing her homework on the dining room table. Every now and again she had looked up from her books, scowling. Nanna Pat seemed very happy, humming as she combed and plaited Sarah's long, fine white-blonde hair.

'You've got such pretty hair, lovey, and you're so dainty. Just like a little fairy.'

Julia had snorted. 'She doesn't look like any of the rest of us though, does she Nanna?'

Sarah snuggled into the protection of Nanna Pat's lap. Julia ran her fingers through her own thick dark curls. 'I've got hair like Mum. You had dark hair as well, didn't you until it went grey?'

'I did lovey. Just like yours and your Mum's. But, you know, we're all different sweetheart and we have to make the best of what we've got.'

She added a pink bow to Sarah's plait. Sarah jumped off Nanna Pat's knee and went into the kitchen to show her Mum, twirling round in her sparkly pink frock and doing a little dance. Her new white patent shoes decorated with a little bow and a stone like a diamond were perfect and she tapped each toe and then her heel and toe the way Miss Musters had taught them at school.

'Sarah Cottle you really look like you're going to be the belle of the ball,' said her Mum, Jane. She had thought it was daft to spend so much on a pair of party shoes when her daughter was bound to grow out of them in a few months, but Sarah had loved them so much, hugging them to her chest and waltzing around the shop and she hadn't had the heart to refuse her.

Sarah was going to her best friend, Amy's, birthday party that afternoon. She felt pretty and happy. When she went back into the living room, Julia had looked up from her homework.

'Sarah come and sit next to me,' she said. Sarah was delighted. Normally her sister seemed too busy to be bothered with her. Her delight turned to horror though as Julia continued, 'I think it's about time you learnt "the awful truth".'

Then she had gone on to tell Sarah that Mum and Dad weren't really her parents at all. That Julia had swapped her on the maternity ward. She said that she hadn't liked the look of her real sister so had switched the identity bracelets.

'So, you have me to thank,' said Julia. 'Because if it hadn't been for me, you'd have had an old woman who looked like a witch for a mother, because your real mother looked just like *Wilma, The Witch With The Wart*. That was a terrifying thought as Sarah was very frightened of *Wilma, The Witch With The Wart*, even though her mum had explained that she was only a puppet and couldn't hurt her and definitely couldn't get out of the television set. Sarah had started to cry.

'That's the last thing you should do,' Julia had

sneered. 'Mum and Dad don't know. You don't want them to suspect the truth because if they find out then you'll have to be swapped back and go and live with the old witch in a nasty hovel, and she'll cut off your hair and sell it. So, you'd just better hope they never find out the truth.'

Suddenly Sarah's world felt like a lonely and scary place and there was no-one she could confide in. No-one must find out "the awful truth".

Jane Cottle was surprised that her daughter was so quiet on the way over to Amy's house but thought maybe she was suddenly nervous about meeting new people. She didn't stay because Amy's Mum was dropping Sarah back later, but she was concerned that her daughter was so pale and uncommunicative on her return. Amy's Mum said that she had been "spooked" by the children's entertainer. And it was true because poor Sarah had been convinced that the jolly fat woman, dressed as a clown, was going to transform her into *Wilma, The Witch With The Wart's* daughter and transport her back to a dreadful hovel. She had fled to the kitchen and cuddled up with Tilda the cat on an old beanbag by the back door.

She seemed so unlike her usual self that Jane took her temperature, but it was quite normal. So, the Calpol was put on hold for the time being. Frank Cottle thought that his daughter might just have got a bit overexcited. She was a sensitive little soul, quite unlike Julia who was robust and confident, and always seemed to be involved in some noisy activity.

Sarah crept around the house like a little ghost. She took to wearing her father's old woollen football hat, the one her mother had accidentally shrunk in the wash. She tucked in all her hair. It felt safer that way and she reasoned that she looked more like the rest of her family if no-one could see her long blonde hair. Initially, her father was delighted. He thought that he might have found a budding companion for his Saturday afternoon outings to the City Ground to watch Nottingham Forest.

Her Mum was less sure. It wasn't so much the hat that worried her but more that Sarah seemed fearful about leaving the house, which indeed she was. Every afternoon at school she would be gripped by the dreadful notion that during the day "the awful truth" would have been discovered and that instead of her mother waiting at the school gates, there would be the woman who looked like *Wilma, The Witch With The Wart* who would lead her back to her horrible hovel.

One day her mother was a few minutes late and arrived to find Sarah sitting sobbing. She wasn't allowed to wear the football hat for school, but she had the hood of her little anorak pulled securely over her head and her arms wrapped tightly around her body. Jane had never seen her daughter so distressed. She made an appointment with Sarah's class teacher who said that Sarah had seemed a bit subdued recently but there appeared to be no specific problems.

Jane asked Julia if she knew of anything that might be upsetting her little sister, but Julia just smiled and said, 'Well, she's different to us, isn't she?' It was true Sarah was small, delicate and blonde with blue eyes whilst Frank, Jane and Julia were big boned and had dark hair and eyes. But Jane Cottle was momentarily a little disturbed by Julia's attitude and reminded her that Sarah was her sister and very special.

In the end Sarah's behaviour was put down to "a stage she was going through". However, because she was only five, this stage in Sarah's life seemed to last for years. In reality, it was only a couple of months and ended the day a miracle happened, when Cousin Sally came back from America. Sally was Mum's cousin, although they hadn't seen each other since they were teenagers, and the amazing thing was that Cousin Sally looked exactly like a grown-up Sarah. Fortunately, Sarah wasn't wearing the football hat because Jane had decreed it, "a bit wiffy and in need of a wash" and thrown it in the laundry basket that morning.

'Why, you're just like me, you little doll,' exclaimed Sally. 'Or at least when I was a young 'un like you.' She had led Sarah over to the full-length mirror in the hall and, sure enough, the likeness was startling.

'You know Sal, I'd forgotten just how blonde you were,' exclaimed Jane.

'Yes, she's more like me than you, but that's

sometimes how it goes in families, but she's got your chin, Janie.'

They had both laughed but were amazed when Sarah started to cry. It was the pure relief. She had sobbed uncontrollably and eventually her mother had taken her up to her bedroom and there at last Sarah told her "the awful truth". Jane Cottle patiently explained the impossibility of Julia's story.

'The moment I first held you, I loved you and knew you were my daughter. I examined every inch of you and saw that little birth mark on your wrist. As for swapping identity bracelets, that is way beyond what a small child could manage, and Julia was barely five when you were born. And there were definitely no mothers on the ward who looked like *Wilma, The Witch With The Wart*.'

Sarah never found out what was said to her sister, but Julia was made to apologise and for a week or so was very quiet and polite to everyone, which was most unusual. Sarah initially felt enormous relief but somehow still had some lingering fears. In the end Frank Cottle, who had been appalled by the whole episode and deeply disappointed in his elder daughter, announced that more drastic action was called for.

'Jane, why don't we put this sorry episode to bed for once and all,' he suggested to his wife. 'Let's get a DNA test done and frame the results. Then Sarah can have a constant reminder that she's definitely a Cottle.'

He was surprised when Jane was less than enthusiastic. 'Frank, the last thing we need to do is make any more of this. No, let's put the whole thing behind us and just keep reassuring her.' She was adamant that she wanted no part in any DNA testing so in the end Frank just had to accept it and things gradually settled down.

\* \* \*

After Sarah had told Nathan the story, he had held her and reassured her that it was totally understandable for a young child to be so terrified.

'But Julia should never have let it go on for so long,' he said.

'In fairness to her, I imagine that a week or so after she told me that story, she would have completely forgotten about it, and I suppose she must have found me very irritating at times. You know more than five years' difference in age is quite an uneasy gap.'

When analysing her relationship with her sister, Sarah had considered that a smaller gap may have meant that in their childhood they would have been playmates and companions and perhaps a bigger gap would have meant that Julia would have been delighted to have a new baby sister who she could take care of. The problem was, Sarah supposed, that she had arrived at a difficult time, just as Julia had started school and was already struggling with the notion that she wasn't after all the most wonderful little girl in the world.

Things had improved a bit when Julia went away to college. When she had returned home at the weekends, Sarah had been struggling as an awkward thirteen-year-old and Julia had seemed glamorous and sophisticated. Julia had lapped up her sister's adoration and for a few years their relationship had been good.

Then Sarah had blossomed into a very attractive young woman, achieved great exam grades and got a place at Manchester Metropolitan University and that seemed to spark all the old petty jealousies as Julia was just emerging from an unhappy long-term relationship and hating everything about her life.

Anyway, for a while, they had seen little of each other but, as she neared the end of her twenties, Julia's life had started to improve. She met Jake who, for no reason Sarah could really understand, appeared to be besotted with her. Julia's confidence soared and she took extra qualifications and actually got a job she enjoyed. She and Jake set up home together, getting a mortgage on a nice little new-build ideally situated for both their jobs. Sarah, in her early twenties, was still finding her feet and struggling a bit with student debt. She was living in a rented flat whilst saving for a deposit and Julia seemed to like nothing better than to drop in and out of her life bringing cast-offs that she "thought might be useful". In reality, some of them were but she just wished that Jules had smaller feet – her sister spent a vast amount on footwear and Sarah would have adored some pre-loved Louboutins, but Julia took a size seven and she a measly four.

However, on balance, she supposed it was good to have a sister; at least as their parents grew older, they could support each other in providing their care. Not that it seemed likely that would be needed anytime soon. In their mid to late fifties, their parents appeared to have boundless energy, although they did seem to be going their own ways much more as the years progressed. Every time they spoke on the phone, Jane Cottle mentioned another weekend away or short break that didn't include Sarah's father, Frank.

Feeling relieved now that Nathan knew the whole story and reassured that she could rely on his support, Sarah was keen for him to be by her side during her sister's visit.

'Julia's popping round late tomorrow afternoon to impart some "big news", so if you come round straight after work, you'll get to meet her for yourself,' she said, giving her boyfriend an extra hug.

\* \* \*

The following day Sarah awaited her sister's visit with a mixture of curiosity and trepidation. There had been a tone to Julia's voice that suggested the big news was not necessarily good news.

Shortly after 6. 00 pm Julia's little red sports car

pulled up outside the flats and Sarah went down to let her in. Sarah explained that Nathan would be joining them when he finished work.

'Oh good,' exclaimed Julia. 'I wanted us to have a few minutes by ourselves.'

Sarah made her sister a coffee and they sat together in the small lounge area. Julia looked very glossy and glamorous, and although Sarah suspected that the almost waist-length dark tresses were not completely natural, the overall impression was one of elegant sophistication.

Julia's ample frame adorned with expensive clothing made the tiny settee look cheap and shabby, and Sarah felt small and scruffy. She hadn't had time to wash her hair for a few days and it was coiled rather listlessly around her head. Her employers' dress code was very relaxed, so she was wearing some well-worn jeans and an oldish sweater and had just navigated a bus journey and a long walk to get back to Withington from the centre of Manchester during rush hour.

'So, what's this "big news" then?' asked Sarah.

'Well, you know Mum's been looking rather glam lately?'

'Er, yes.'

'There is a reason, and his name is Paul and apparently, they've been having some sort of clandestine affair on and off for years.'

For a moment Sarah was speechless. She had realised that her parents were spending less time together over recent years, but this news was totally shocking and unexpected. Throughout her childhood her parents had provided a stable and loving environment for their children. It seemed almost impossible that their relationship was anything but monogamous.

'Did Mum actually tell you that, and how is Dad taking all this?'

'Well, that's just the thing, Sarah. I know you don't see as much of them as I do, but you've probably guessed they've been gradually drifting apart over the last few years. So, in a way, I'm not surprised and actually Dad, outwardly anyway, is pretty buoyant about the whole thing. I'm not sure if he was joking, but he did say he might do a bit of travelling and come back with a nice young bride. So, who knows?

'But, Julia, I can't believe that Mum's been seeing someone else for years. Did you ever suspect anything?'

'Well, not exactly and I do think she went to great pains to provide us with a stable home life and never arouse any suspicions. I suppose now she feels that we're older and have our own lives and can cope. By the way, Dad isn't quite the innocent in all of this. He did have a fling a while back, and I suppose that sort of helped to bring Mum's affair out into the open.'

Sarah felt confused and excluded. So, her Mum had been having a clandestine affair for years, and her father had enjoyed some sort of fling. It felt like her world was crumbling. She couldn't speak;

she was fighting back the tears.

Julia saw her expression and reached across to take her hand. 'Sarah, his infidelity was nothing much. Just a one night stand, I think, and Mum tried to play it down. She didn't want you to know because she would have realised you'd have been upset, but I suppose it finally gave her the freedom to follow her heart.'

Sarah was surprised by her sister's concern. Sometimes Julia seemed so blasé and unfeeling, but suddenly she realised that this was probably some sort of coping mechanism.

'So, have you met this Paul? What's he like?' she managed.

'Now therein lies another story. The amazing thing is that Mum was showing me some photos of him and I realised that he was someone I remembered meeting as a child years ago. I was only young. I think Mum was pregnant with you. We were sitting in the park and then this man turned up and Mum went all quiet and flustered. She told me to go off and play and I did. For the first few minutes Mum was looking over at me on the swings and waving, but then when I looked over, she and the man were deep in conversation. I got a bit bored and crept away from the main play area and round the back of where they were sitting. They hadn't seen me approach, and I saw they were holding hands. The minute they realised I was back they sort of sprang apart, and Mum said we must go because she'd promised to buy me an ice-cream. As we walked away, I asked her why she'd been holding the man's hand. She said it was because he was sad, and she was comforting him, but that it was nothing for me to worry about. I asked her who he was, but she just said it was someone who'd come to feed the ducks, and she didn't really know him.'

Sarah was amazed; it appeared that this affair had actually begun before she was even born. Her parents' apparently cosy relationship was unravelling by the minute.

Julia took a sip of her coffee before continuing. 'Well, I don't suppose I would have remembered him, but he turned up a few more times in the park after that, although I never caught them holding hands again. I suppose I noticed him because he had a beard, and I didn't know many men with beards, and he just looked different to other men I knew at the time. I think I expected all men to be like Dad and Grandad Jim and Grandpa – big and loud and going bald and, well, he wasn't like that.'

Sarah was intrigued. 'So have you got a photo on your phone?' She couldn't wait to see what this Paul looked like.

'I haven't but you'll get to meet him soon. Well, I hope you and Nathan will because Mum's very keen for us all to meet up, and she wants me and Jake, you and Nathan and her and Paul to get together for a meal. So, I'm going to try and organise that. But I will send over a photo if you like. Mum emailed me a few, so I'll email you a couple later.'

'Well, we'll be sure to be there. I'm most interested to meet him. But what you were saying about seeing him and remembering him from years ago; did you say anything to Mum about that?'

'I did,' said Julia. 'She didn't say much about it, but just said it was likely that it was him. That she had known him for a long time, but there had been a good many years when they had hardly seen each other. She did stress that she had really wanted everything to work out for her and Dad, and it had until we left home and then apparently, when Dad was unfaithful, it sort of brought things to a head, but now they've fairly amicably decided to go their own ways.' She paused and looked critically at her sister. 'You OK, Sarah, you look a bit pale?'

'Well, it has come as a bit of a shock, Jules.'

'Yes, I know, it's a lot to take in, but I honestly think both Mum and Dad will find happiness now. Mum and Paul have a lot in common apparently; that's how they got back together - through some Northern Soul reunions and things just progressed from there. Now when is Nathan going to put in an appearance?'

Just then Nathan bounded up the stairs, knocking briefly on the flat door and then flinging it open in his usual enthusiastic manner. Sarah went over to hug him and made the introductions.

'Well Nathan, hasn't Sarah done well for herself?' purred Julia. 'She didn't tell me you were so handsome. You look like you work out.'

Nathan was obviously delighted with the flattery. Sarah thought he was gorgeous, but he wasn't really conventionally handsome and certainly unused to female adoration. Sarah didn't think that her sister would really be his type, for one thing she towered over him in her heels, but she thought any man would be flattered by the attention of such a stunning woman. Also, it was true, Nathan did work out and, unlike Sarah, was quite sporty, as was Julia. Sarah fought hard to maintain a pleasant expression as they discussed their various athletic activities. She hadn't been aware that Julia still played netball or that she had once almost played at county level. She was relieved when Julia said she must be going as she and Jake were going out for a meal.

'Sarah, I'll get back to you on that restaurant booking, and I'll send you a picture of Paul. Oh, yes, I almost forgot. Jake's got me a new set of saucepans, so I've bought you my old ones. They're a bit heavy, but maybe this fit young man can bring them up from the car.' She grabbed Nathan's arm and he was forced to follow her as she clattered down the stairs in her expensive, red-soled shoes, leaving a trail of exotic musky perfume in her wake.

Sarah stood at the window watching Julia unloading boxes from the car boot. At one point she lent close to Nathan and seemed to be whispering something into his ear. In turn he enveloped her in a brief hug. Sarah was relieved when he picked up the boxes and made his way back up to the flat.

Later that evening Sarah's phone pinged to announce the arrival of the photos. She had explained the "big news" to Nathan and that she was eagerly awaiting the images.

'I'm going to get them up on the PC,' she announced. 'Let's have a really good look at him.'

There were a couple of photographs, one of Jane Cottle holding Paul's hand in a holiday location, and one, a more posed shot of him, perhaps taken a number of years previously. Sarah enlarged the solo image as much as she could. Paul was small, blond and blue-eyed. He seemed to have lost the beard over the years.

'Er Nathan,' she asked, 'does he look like anyone you know?'

Nathan came over, pulling up the spare chair to sit beside her. 'What did you think when Julia told you the news?' he asked.

'Well, of course, I was terribly shocked and really couldn't believe it had been going on for so long, but,' she glanced back at the image on the screen and pulled a strand of her blond hair contemplatively, 'I didn't actually put two and two together.' She clutched Nathan's hand, whispering, 'It could just be a coincidence, couldn't it?'

'It could, but,' he paused and squeezed her hand, 'Julia had a quick word with me when I went down to collect those saucepans.'

'I know,' Sarah laughed, 'I was watching from the window.'

'Well, she may have been flirting with me up here, but down by the car it was nothing like that. In fact, I'll tell you exactly what she said because it surprised me a little bit, but it might be good for you to know.'

'Go on,' said Sarah, 'let's hear what she said behind my back.'

'She said, "I'm glad Sarah's got you. She's a sensitive soul and she may need a little extra support at the moment. Please give her a bit of special care, and if you can, remind her that I'm truly always there for her".'

'She said that?' Sarah was astonished.

'She did and, you know what, I really think she meant it. Let's face it, sometimes the truth isn't as awful as we think it's going to be.'

# NEIGHBOURHOOD WATCH

Connie was surprised to hear someone knocking at the door. They had only moved into the house the previous week and she didn't really know anyone. She had spoken to the young couple next door and they were friendly enough, but she was pretty sure they were out at work all day and she wasn't expecting any deliveries.

When she opened the door, she saw that the caller was a middle-aged woman with a clipboard. Connie hoped that she wasn't going to try and sell her anything, but she didn't look like someone canvassing for double-glazing. She was quite formally dressed in a dark red suit with a loose mac over the top and was actually wearing white gloves.

She beamed at Connie and held out her hand, saying, 'Hello, I hope I haven't called at an inconvenient time. My name is Margaret Stansfield and my husband and I run the local Neighbourhood Watch group. We try and encourage all newcomers to join. It's so important to keep the area safe and secure and encourage everyone to be vigilant.'

Connie was nodding and smiling. She couldn't place the woman's accent, but somehow it didn't sound natural; almost as though she was putting on a posh telephone voice as her mother used to do. But she was all for keeping the area safe and keen to get to know other residents in the street.

'Of course. Me and my husband are all for that. In fact, he's just out now buying a padlock for the back gate.' She indicated the shared passageway at the side of the house which led to the high wooden gates which allowed access to theirs and the neighbours' back gardens. She liked the fact that she and Alan had downsized to a mid-link terraced property. It felt nice, safe, and secure and should be easy to maintain.

Margaret greeted this news with great enthusiasm. 'That's what we like to hear. I'm sure we can count on your support then. May I just take a few details from you so that we can add you onto our email list and make sure you get our newsletters and invites to our monthly meetings?'

'Of course,' said Connie. She invited Margaret in. She stepped into the hall but refused to go into the kitchen to sit down, saying that this was to be a brief introductory visit as she didn't want to impose on Connie so soon after she had moved in.

'What a lovely house,' said Margaret. 'I'm sure you'll be very happy here. It's such a nice, friendly neighbourhood.'

Connie agreed that it appeared to be. She supplied their email address and telephone number. It was nice to have met another neighbour and good to know that there was an active Neighbourhood Watch scheme in the area.

Margaret passed her a glossy leaflet, outlining the benefits of Neighbourhood Watch.

'Are your contact details on it?' asked Connie turning the leaflet over.

'Oh, silly me,' said Margaret. 'I meant to give you one with our little card attached. I'll pop one through your letterbox in a few minutes. Now I hope you don't think I'm being cheeky, but would you mind if I used your bathroom. I've been out on Neighbourhood Watch business all morning and I don't think I can wait until I get back home.' She laughed, seeming a little embarrassed and looked up the stairs expectantly.

'Of course,' said Connie. 'But we've got a downstairs loo just through the utility room, so please use that.'

'Oh, how useful,' said Margaret as Connie showed her through.

When she came out of the cloakroom, she seemed very keen to leave. 'Must get back,' she said. 'I have to let the dog out. I'll pop by with the little card shortly.'

Just after she had gone Alan returned with the padlock.

'We've had a visitor,' said Connie. 'Neighbourhood Watch lady.'

'That's nice,' said Alan. 'Where does she live then?'

'Do you know,' said Connie, 'she didn't tell me, but we'll find out soon because she's going to drop a little card round.'

Alan went out into the garden to sort out the padlock. A few moments later he returned looking a bit worried.

'Con, have you seen the mower?' he asked. 'Did you move it somewhere?'

'No,' said Connie. 'Why would I move it? It was on the back lawn last time I saw it.'

'Well, it's not there now,' said Alan.

Connie was perplexed. She went out with Alan onto the small square of back garden, but the new lawn mower was nowhere to be seen.

'Surely we can't have been burgled,' said Connie. 'I've been here all the time.'

'Well, that's the only explanation,' said Alan. 'I'd better call the police and report it. Not that they'll be able to do much about it, I wouldn't think. The thief and my mower will be long gone by now. Gone without a trace.'

'I'll let that Neighbourhood Watch woman know as well,' said Connie, 'as soon as I get her details. She can alert the neighbours then.'

* * *

Margaret (aka Maggie Mayfield) got into the white van that Gerry had parked down the road. She pulled off the white gloves and sighed.

'Let's get out of here Gez,' she said. 'Bit of a let-down. Wanted to get a look upstairs, but she had a downstairs loo. Still, these might be worth something.' She pulled a couple of tiny figurines out of her pocket. She had found them on the shelf in the downstairs cloakroom.

'Yeah,' agreed Gerry. 'Not much of a haul, but I did get a mower that looks new. Might be able to make a few quid out of it at the car boot on Sunday. Anyway, let's hotfoot it over to Bradford this afternoon. I think we need to put a few miles between us and this town.'

Maggie settled back contentedly in her seat and took off her grey wig to give her head a good scratch. It was a horrible-looking thing but a great disguise along with the charity shop suit and mac, and vile clumpy shoes.

The Neighbourhood Watch scam had been her brainwave; but it was true she and Gerry did watch neighbourhoods. They travelled around in their van, looking out for properties that had recently been sold. People weren't as careful when they had just moved home, and they generally didn't know many of their neighbours. They were keen to speak to a friendly soul and easily distracted. The thing was to move on quickly and not to visit the same area twice.

\* \* \*

'Anyway,' asked Alan, 'what's young Harry been doing?' He was referring to their young grandson who was visiting for the day. He was an engaging but slightly unusual child who loved clocks and numbers and record-keeping of any sort. Earlier that day Alan had given him a small notebook and told him how he used to record car number plates.

'Not many young folks do it nowadays, but you might enjoy it,' Alan had said. 'Why don't you go into my office. You can sit at my desk and look out of the window. It's quite a busy road, lots of traffic going past. You can record the times and number plates and type of vehicles.' He was keen to keep Harry occupied whilst he was out. Connie was still busy unpacking boxes and he thought she was looking rather tired.

Harry hadn't seemed too excited by the idea, although he liked sitting in Alan's office chair, pretending he was an executive. But after a while he had got bored and was just about to go down and ask his grannie if he could have a snack when a posh-sounding lady had come to the door. He had leaned over the banisters to try and hear what she was saying but it didn't seem very interesting, and he knew better than to interrupt when his grannie had visitors. He went back into the small front bedroom that his grandad was using for an office and picked up the notebook. He decided that he would have a go at the number plate collecting thing.

He started by writing down the numbers of all the vehicles parked in the street. He saw a thin man with a lot of tattoos on his arms carrying a lawnmower coming out of the alleyway between grandad and grandma's house and their neighbours. He guessed it must be one of the neighbours. He walked down the street and put the mower into the back of the van. Harry wrote down the number of the white van along with the numbers of the other vehicles parked in the street. Then he thought he would make it a bit more interesting by putting a few more details down. He got his grandad's ruler and drew some columns and put in more information. Then he began to record the details of other cars and vans as they drove through the street.

Across the road a courier was making a delivery. Harry wished he knew what was in the big brown box that the man was passing to the woman on the doorstep. He wondered if it was anything to eat. He was getting hungry. He was glad when he heard his grannie showing the posh-sounding lady out of the house. He watched her walk down the path and out onto the street. He thought she looked a bit strange with her tightly curled grey hair and big coat and those gloves. Perhaps, he thought, she was really old and felt the cold. His grannie said that old people felt the cold because their bones were thinner and they couldn't move about so quickly. He was surprised when he saw her get into the white van that the man had put the mower in. They didn't match somehow, the skinny man with the tattoos and the old lady, but perhaps he was her son. The car sped off. Harry recorded the time it left the street.

Then he heard his grandad come in. Unusually for him, he sounded a bit cross. Perhaps it would cheer him up to know that Harry had used the notebook he had given him. Harry hopped down the stairs. He liked the stairs. At home they lived in a bungalow, so stairs were a bit of a novelty.

Harry ran into the kitchen to give his grandad a hug. He proudly produced the small notebook. 'Grandad,' he said, 'do you want to look at my car numbers?'

Alan took the notebook. He was impressed with the amount of effort Harry had put into the exercise, especially when he came to the entry – BL17 JKO, white van, man with mower and posh lady, 11. 30 am.

# DYING BREATH

The building is bleak and grey. It was cheaply constructed of pre-cast concrete blocks in the mid-60s back when little thought was given to aesthetic appeal. Entry is through a steel door via a key-pad system; the codes change frequently, every time an employee is dismissed. The public are forbidden to enter. All claims and enquiries are dealt with over the telephone by a small army of euphemistically described Customer Care Agents. The Agents are clustered over five floors identically populated by twelve blocks of four desks per floor. Each block is divided in the centre by acoustic screens, but every Agent hears the constant babble of their colleagues delivering the mandatory script along with the loud beep which announces each incoming call.

On the third floor in the second right-hand block one of the workstations is empty. Team Leader Trudy frowns and checks with HR, but Julie Marshall has not rung in. She looks across her desk and sees that Julie's friend, Debbie, has just finished a claim.

'No sign of your partner in crime yet then?' she asks.

Debbie looks around and realises that her friend hasn't come in, but before she can respond there is a loud beep in her headset, and she is battling with another call. It's going to be a long one because she will need to engage help from the Language Line to complete the claim. Now and again, over the next hour, she looks to her right but there is no sign of Julie. She begins to be concerned.

The two women have become close over the last year or so. They are the oldest on the team, waiting out retirement really, though in reality, with the State Pension changes, it may be ten years or so until they can hang up their headsets. In the meantime, they buoy up each other's spirits by finding humour where they can. Debbie is bright and bubbly, small and curvy with a silver pixie cut and a wicked wit. Julie is more serious but slender and smart with a glossy dark bob and an appreciation of her friend's sometimes vaguely obscene interpretations of the phonetic alphabet.

Trudy wonders what the two women find to laugh about. She thinks they're a strange pair, getting dressed up to come to work and not seeming to care whether they achieve promotion – which they won't, she thinks – too old and slow. Whereas she worked her way up to a Team Leader's post as soon as she could. It means she doesn't have to take calls anymore. No, Trudy's job is to keep an eye on the team, helping ensure that they comply with the regulations and meet the ever-changing targets set by management. She shrugs on the ancient woolly brown cardigan that she keeps on the back of her office chair. It goes nicely with her selection of beige and fawn workwear. She thinks those two must spend a fortune getting their hair done. She doesn't bother. Her sister trims it every six weeks or so, and it's just the right length to pull into a ponytail.

\* \* \*

On the other side of the city in a side-room on the geriatric ward of the General Hospital, Julie sits by her mother's bed, holding her small frail hand and sobbing. She'd arrived at the hospital after her mother had lapsed into unconsciousness. The young doctor was kind but firm. The CT scans had been examined carefully and her mother would not regain consciousness. Following a fall, she has sustained a subdural haematoma, 'bleeding onto the brain,' the doctor clarified. Given her age and frailty, and after discussion with colleagues, the decision has been made that surgery is inappropriate. He assures Julie that her mother is in no pain and that she will just 'slip away peacefully.' Julie wants her mother to open her eyes and look at her one last time.

She squeezes her age-spotted hand, saying, 'Come on Mum, wake up and say something nasty to me.'

Julie is glad that the young doctor has left the room. She is not sure that he would appreciate or understand her comment. The truth is that her relationship with her mother has deteriorated over the last few years and on more than one occasion Julie has been ordered to 'keep your nose out of my affairs.'

Her mother much prefers her brother, but he lives too far away to reach the hospital in time to hold her hand as she "slips away", so it will be the daughter that she lately seems to despise who will assume this duty.

Her mother is still breathing in loud irregular bursts. Julie squeezes her hand more tightly. It seems impossible that after 88 years she will be gone. She is tiny and pale in the hospital bed, with her brown and grey hair messily strewn on the pillow. She has never been robust, suffering numerous aches and pains, but surviving heart surgery a few years previously and approaching life with a furious self-centred determination. She has become increasingly unpleasant to deal with, but Julie appreciates her courage following Julie's father's death a few years ago. So cruel that, when they are most needed, life partners are gone leaving their spouses lonely and isolated, struggling to complete everyday tasks.

Her mother's breathing becomes progressively noisy and irregular. For a moment it seems to stop completely. Then with a gasp it restarts.

A nurse looks in. 'Still holding on, lovey?' she asks kindly.

Julie nods. She looks across at the clock on the wall. It is almost eight thirty. She has been at the hospital for five hours and should have been at work thirty minutes ago. She supposes she could ring them on her mobile, but she doesn't want to let go of her mother's hand and anyway work seems meaningless and irrelevant as she sits by her mother's bedside.

If Julie's partner had still been around then he could have contacted people and helped sort things out, but they split up last year. So now he has no responsibility for her or her for him and, generally, she is pleased about this situation, but just at this moment she feels terribly alone. There will be so many things that she will have to handle all by herself. No doubt her brother will turn up at some point but she knows from bitter experience that she will be expected to take overall responsibility for all necessary arrangements. This has always been the situation. Her brother has been the clever, charming but feckless one whilst she, as the older sibling, has been expected to be reliable and take charge.

Then, with a shudder, her mother takes what will be her dying breath. For a moment Julie is startled. She hasn't let go of her mother's hand, but she was so weary that for a while she has been lost in her own thoughts and almost nodded off. She realises that the hand in hers is now cold and limp, but she doesn't want to let go; she will never be able to hold that hand again.

A short while later the kind nurse returns and gently removes her mother's hand from Julie's.

'We'll take care of her now,' she says, respectfully placing the hand on top of the bed on the clean white sheet. She takes Julie into a small sitting room and brings her a cup of tea.

\* \* \*

Trudy attends the morning debrief. 'Just one absent today, Julie Marshall. I don't know the reason. She was due on at eight, but no phone call so far.'

'Not like her,' says Monica, the Deputy Call Centre Manager.

Trudy sniffs. She isn't Julie's greatest fan ever since she overheard her complaining about the mandatory script to a colleague. 'Well, she seems to have lost a bit of motivation recently, and her average call handling times are becoming unacceptably high. If she's going to start taking unauthorised leave, perhaps we need to look at disciplinary action.'

'Is that her file?' asks Monica, gesturing to the manilla folder in Trudy's hands. 'Can I have a look?'

Trudy reaches to pass the file over, but all at once she feels a sharp twinge of pain in her back between her shoulder blades, almost as if she's being jabbed very hard by a fingertip. For a moment she loosens her grip on the file and it falls to the floor, scattering its contents. Embarrassed, Trudy bends down to pick up the paperwork, but strangely she seems to have lost control of her hands and fumbles around helplessly. The air around her suddenly feels very cold and there is a high-pitched buzzing in her ears. Clumsily, she manages to stuff the papers untidily back into the file, but her knees appear to have locked and for a second or two she can't get up. Panic seizes her. Whatever is wrong with her? She despises weakness and hysteria but realises that all she wants to do is sit on the floor and howl.

'Trudy, are you OK?' Monica is concerned. She wonders if Trudy is having some sort of stroke or episode. Privately, she's always thought her overweight and unfit, but Trudy has often boasted that she is, "disgustingly healthy", a claim that Monica finds vulgar and clichéd.

Then the buzzing in her ears ceases and Trudy is back on her feet. 'I'm fine,' she tells Monica, but she can't imagine what just happened. She promises herself that she'll get her blood pressure checked out; her sister suffers from hypertension and people say that these things often run in families. But, for now, she feels fine if slightly shaken, and just needs to have a few minutes alone to gather her wits.

'I'll leave it with you,' she says to Monica, indicating the file. 'I know you're probably a bit busy right now.'

Trudy nips into the fifth-floor ladies' toilet. Her reflection looks reassuringly normal, just rather flustered, and it doesn't appear that she's suffering any ill-effects. She washes her hands, straightens her cardigan and re-does her ponytail. But then she is startled as, turning away from the sink, she glimpses the reflection of a shadowy shape moving behind her in the mirror. But when she looks back it is gone. What a strange day she is having. Then a thought occurs to her. She had a prawn curry for tea the previous evening. She wonders if a weird type of seafood allergy could be responsible. She takes her pulse – it does seem a little raised. Very odd; she normally has such a robust constitution.

Julie's mother leaves the room. She's quite enjoying walking through doors and walls, floating a little above the floor. It's very restful and there is no pain at all now in her hips, knees, or neck. That wretched tinnitus has gone too, and she can hear every sound so distinctly. Her vision is crystal clear; the colours around her bright and vibrant – no cataracts to contend with. *I Can See Clearly Now,* she hums the tune to the Johnny Nash song of which Julie used to be so fond as a child.

It is great to be invisible and whilst, as a spirit, the impact she can make on her environment is limited, her burst of anger at Trudy's comments was sufficient to  stimulate a spike of spiritual energy. That gave the woman a nasty shock! She giggles when she remembers the look of confusion on Trudy's spiteful face. What a dreadful place. Her poor Julie. No wonder she sometimes seems to lack vitality and joy.

Anyway, now her daughter is in for a nice surprise. Yes, there be sadness and a bit of chaos ahead, but Julie won't have to work in that soul-destroying job anymore – soon she will be free to follow her creative dreams with a nice little inheritance at her disposal. Julie's mother floats down the concrete steps, out through the steel Call Centre door into the clear autumn air.

# BLIND DATE

'So how did the date go?' Helen caught me up as I entered the flats, a huge laundry basket in her arms.

'Let me take that for you Helen.'

Whilst not exactly elderly, Helen was around 30 years older than me and sometimes walked with the aid of a stick. Reluctantly, she passed the basket over and hobbled up the stairs, calling out that she would put the kettle on, and I could tell her all about my date over a coffee if I had time.

The coffee and accompanying chocolate biscuit were very welcome. I tried to make my story as entertaining as possible, but the truth was that the date had not been a success.

'Well, he turned up late, wearing flip-flops and looking a good 15 years older than his picture and then talked incessantly about himself. In fact, in the end I just couldn't stand it anymore. Told him I had a migraine, thanked him for his company and left as quickly as I could.'

Helen laughed. 'Well Emma, I think you were just unlucky. I'm sure the next one will be better.'

'I don't know. I'm beginning to think that online dating really isn't for me. It seems so false somehow.'

'In my day it was blind dating and that really

was a minefield. No photos or information or texts or anything; usually a date arranged by a well-meaning friend. But, amazingly, it worked for me.'

I looked at Helen in surprise. It was the last thing I had expected to hear.

'Yes, I met John on a blind date, and we were married for nearly 40 years.'

'Really, Helen.' I looked towards John's photo on the windowsill. I had never met him. He had died a few years before Helen had moved into the flat but whenever she spoke about him it was with such love that it was obvious that theirs had been a wonderful marriage.

'But that first date wasn't exactly a success. I knew though. I knew he was the one that I wanted to spend the rest of my life with. The thing was I was so afraid that he wouldn't even want to see me again.'

I was intrigued and begged Helen to tell me the full story. 'Are you sitting comfortably,' she asked with a smile, 'then I'll begin.'

*I was really out of my depth in London. I'd lived in the north of England all my young life, but, although I was quiet and shy, I'd always dreamed of a more interesting and cosmopolitan lifestyle. Then someone told me about a scheme where you could go to London and be recruited by an agency that would put you up in a flatshare with other young girls and find you an office job. I went for an interview and was accepted. Of course, I was accepted. I imagine almost everyone* was. Anyway, it wasn't great. It was hard sharing a flat with three people you didn't know, and I even had to share a bedroom. The other girls seemed more confident than me and had established themselves quickly. I did get a job but it was dreary and repetitive. The weekends were the worst. London is a horrible place to be if you don't have much money. The first few weekends I saw all the sights on my own.

It was a lonely old experience and then one of the girls in my office, Margie, took pity on me and invited me to share lunch with her a time or two. She realised that I didn't really have any friends in London and arranged a date for me with her cousin, John, who'd recently been in a relationship, but something had gone wrong and now he was at a bit of a loose end. She assured me that he was really nice, and good-looking. I didn't have high hopes, but my weekends were dire. What had I got to lose? I let her set me up with a blind date with him, meeting for a Saturday lunch-time drink and snack.

I was really surprised when I got to the pub. Well, for a start it wasn't a pub as I knew them. It was very smart and trendy but John, he was absolutely gorgeous. I was a bit dowdy at the time. I was young and slim with long dark hair, but I had no confidence and very few social skills. Also, I didn't have much money and, in those days, very little style. I remember being very conscious of my down-at-heel boots and my rather shabby mac; it had seemed fashionable when I bought it but, like most cheap garments, it didn't improve with continuous wear, which was what it got as it was either that or a short furry jacket. I didn't possess any other outerwear at the time.

Well, we had a lager each and a sandwich. He really was nice as well as good-looking and did try to get me talking about myself and looked interested in what I had to say but, for the life of me, I couldn't actually think of anything to say. My life really was dull and I didn't do much besides go to work and come home and have a lonely bit of supper. He, on the other hand, seemed to have established himself in the city and talked happily about friends and pubs and music gigs. That was one thing we did have in common – I loved music – rock, blues, folk – but I hadn't the confidence to go to a music event by myself and because I was so keen to make a good impression, I was quite tongue-tied and found myself mumbling incoherently about favourite artists and songs. He was very much the gentleman, wouldn't let me pay for my drink or sandwich.

I debated whether to offer to buy a round, but I was conscious of the fact that I was not scintillating company and didn't want him to feel trapped into spending another half an hour with me – that was how low my self-esteem was at that moment. Anyway, before I could decide, he asked me if I wanted another but seemed relieved when I politely declined and quickly followed with the offer to walk me to the tube station. So, I picked up my bag and we headed out the door towards the nearest underground. He held the door open for me, but didn't take my arm or anything. I liked walking along next to him. Just for a moment *it felt more like I belonged in the city, but I knew it was going to be a short-lived feeling and suddenly my one desire was to prolong the date and my contact with John at all costs. I hatched a half-baked plan. Fumbling in my lime green fringed suede shoulder bag – went with nothing but held everything and my only handbag anyway - I let out an exclamation of despair as I rootled around, seemingly fruitlessly.*

*'Oh, no. I can't believe it. I can't find my purse.'*

*John caught my arm, turning me towards him, his face full of concern.*

*'Let's find a seat and then you can have a proper look.' He patted my bulging shoulder bag. 'It's bound to be in there somewhere. You'd have needed it on the outward journey.'*

*I had to think quickly. 'No, you see I always put the tube fare in my coat pocket before I come out. I hate to have to fumble around when I get into the station and everyone's rushing around.' This actually wasn't true. I always fumbled around, much to all the other passengers' consternation.*

*Anyway, we found a bench and he sat there patiently whilst I started taking things out of my bag and making a big thing of feeling in all the corners whilst actually making sure that my little purse remained firmly at the bottom of that big bag. What a good thing it was a little purse. It only held cash you see. In the 70s you didn't pay by debit card or on your phone or anything. You paid by cash or sometimes a cheque for big purchases. You did have a cheque guarantee card but mine was kept along with my* passport in my top drawer. Every week I just took out the cash from the bank that I needed for that week. So, my purse probably held about ten pounds. So, whilst the loss of ten pounds in the mid-70s was upsetting, it wasn't like losing a wallet stuffed with credit and debit cards. All the same, I didn't really want John to think I had been the victim of a pickpocket or anything that required police intervention.

'I was in a bit of a rush to come out,' I mumbled. 'Probably left it at home. Look, I hate to ask this, but could you possibly lend me a couple of pounds. I will let you have it back next week and,' I added bravely, 'if you have time, I could buy you a drink and snack to say thank you as well.'

Being the good guy he was, John had immediately thrust a five-pound note into my hand.

'I promise I'll pay you back and thank you so much. Are you OK for next Saturday in the same place at one'?

John had nodded and after getting an assurance from me that I would be OK and report the loss to the Police if my purse didn't turn up at home, hurried off in the opposite direction.

I really wondered if I would see him again. I half expected him to send a message through Margie saying that he couldn't make Saturday lunchtime, but we were very busy at work and only saw each other a couple of times in passing. She asked me how the date had gone, and I gave her a thumbs-up sign. I wondered what his version had been. I breathed a sigh of relief when Friday evening came round and there *was no message.*

*I was much better prepared the following Saturday. I had steeled myself for disappointment and decided I would treat myself to a cinema outing if John didn't materialise. Luckily, my birthday was coming up and I had received a very welcome postal order from my parents. I had a hair appointment that morning and bought myself a new top and the weather was mild enough to wear my good shoes and my short fluffy jacket instead of the dismal mac. I had racked my brains for interesting musical titbits and treated my eyes to an extra layer of liner and mascara. So, all eventualities were catered for.*

*I arrived at the pub with just five minutes to spare and looked around anxiously. He was not there but determinedly I made my way to the bar and ordered two halves of lager and found a small table near the window. If he didn't arrive, I would drink both halves before my lonely cinema outing and send the five pounds back through Margie on Monday. It was five past one and I was decided on that course of action when John burst through the door, red in the face, clutching a carrier bag.*

*Our second date was a completely different story. John was so relieved to hear that my purse had been recovered safe and sound in my flat. Apparently, he had feared that I had been the victim of theft and left traumatised in the lonely city. His carrier bag contained a small handbag that he felt would provide better control of my belongings, and he'd been delayed because he'd been bargaining for it in a second-hand* shop.

'It's a bit scruffy,' he said, 'but you did mention you liked purple.' I have it to this day.

Over the coming weeks we saw more and more of each other, and I learnt that, although John was confident and popular, he understood that London was a big and lonely place.

'I had my brother for company when I first arrived,' he said. 'I think you're very brave. I worried about you and was so pleased to see you again. I rang Margie at work but, well you know what she's like. She just said you were fine, and she didn't really know you all that well and didn't have a number for you.'

For my part, I got Margie a big box of chocolates and thanked her for the introduction. She just shrugged and said, 'thought you'd get on. He's a bit soft, just like you.' And so he was.

Helen reached up and took a letter down from the mantlepiece. 'Do you know it's my birthday next week and every year I get one of these.'

I looked questioningly at her.

'Yes,' she went on. 'That was the sort of person John was and still is to me. Every birthday I get a card from him. You see before he died, and he knew he was dying; he wrote ten birthday cards to me. He numbered them and put a little kiss on the back.' She turned the envelope over to show me. 'He arranged with his nephew that they would be posted out to me in numbered order just before each of my birthdays. I know because the first one contained a letter explaining what he had planned. I know it sounds corny and a bit like that film.'

'*PS I Love You*', I said. 'No, it's a lovely and thoughtful idea, and a wonderful caring thing to do.'

'This is number eight. So, he plans I have two more years left in me.' She laughed and continued, 'They do bring me joy though. Each one contains a little poem and the cards are really beautiful. I can't imagine where he found them or how he had the strength to organise them all really.'

'I suppose it must have given him some final comfort,' I said, 'to think of you receiving something lovely when he was no longer around.'

'One thing though,' Helen sighed. 'I never did tell him I lied to him about the purse. He was such an honest, straight-forward soul. I just couldn't risk him changing his mind about me. But I'm really not sorry I did it. We were so happy and had so many wonderful years together. Now get back on that computer and find your Mr Right. I know he's out there somewhere waiting for you.'

# FROZEN IN TIME

Sorry I didn't get here this morning, Codie, but I've been a bit busy. One of my buddies needed some support. You might remember him. Zane, Zane Payne. Used to live in our zone. We were in the same Education Network. I think you had a bit of a thing for him at one time. Most of the girls did; still do by all accounts. He comes across as a "flash git", in the words of our great-grandpa, but he's not that bad really. I remember going to his apartment a time or two when we were kids. He was spoilt beyond belief. Well in some ways he was. Lovely bedroom, every gadget and gizmo under the sun, but his parents' interest in him seemed a bit superficial somehow and I got the feeling he was lonely at home. He was an only child. Maybe if he'd had a sister like you, he would have turned out a lot different. Who knows?

Anyway, me and old Zaney still get together from time to time and a couple of days ago he asked me to meet him at The Hitchcock Bar. Said if we didn't meet up soon it would be a very long time before he could see me again. When I'd asked him why he told me some weird story about going on a cryogenically induced break for 15 years. *Intriguing*, I'd thought. *Weird, even by Zane's standards.*

So, I'd rocked up to The Hitchcock and there was my man quaffing back some ridiculous-looking pink drink.

'What in Zoot's name is that?' I'd asked.

'Double gin and rose petal infused tonic,' Zane had replied, holding up the glass and looking fondly at its contents.

'Not very manly, mate,' I'd observed.

'Real men embrace their feminine side, and I have absolutely no insecurities about my manliness.'

'You don't seem to have any insecurities about anything, but, seriously, aren't you a bit scared about this whole cryogenic business? What if it goes wrong? What if you never wake up? What if the world ends or we get invaded, and you get destroyed?'

'Ah, Corban, life is full of uncertainties, but I do know something. Although we can't stop the ageing process, advances in cryogenics give us the opportunity to suspend it.'

'So, what's the benefit? You're going to wake up in a world you don't know. All your mates are going to belong to a different generation. Surely it makes sense just to grow old gracefully, or . . . ,' I'd laughed, 'in your case disgracefully.'

'Look, it's different for you. I can see that. You've got a wife and kids. You're gonna want to see them grow up and in some ways, as you get older, you'll be living life through them. But me, I've just got my fading looks and a career that seems to have ground to a standstill.'

'From where I'm standing, you seem to be doing pretty well. What about Lanae? I'd thought you two might be moving onto something permanent.'

'You know, that's another thing. I don't seem to fancy women of my own age anymore and I think things have got a bit stale with me and Lanae. She's coming up for 39 soon and keeps hinting that she wants us to make a family unit. But it's not for me and, let's be honest, there's nothing to stop her having children by herself. For Zoot's sake this is 2084, we're not living at the beginning of the millennium!'

'Well, you could do a lot worse. She's a beautiful woman and most importantly seems to be besotted with you.'

'And maybe that's the reason. I like a challenge. I crave excitement and variety. Anyway, I thought maybe you might have guessed there was someone else in my life – actually two someone elses in my life.'

'So, won't you have regrets about leaving them?'

'One is Lanae's cousin, Rosa. She's a little younger than Lanae and I must admit it was exciting when we first got together, but now, I don't know. We don't seem to have so much fun anymore. The thing is I've also met another lovely young woman, Nella, whom I'm particularly drawn to.'

'So, doesn't she feel the same?'

'She does at the moment, but she's only 28. She

is young and beautiful, and I think very attracted to me, but I doubt she'll feel the same when I start to lose my looks. That's the other thing; I think my ratings have gone down recently. VisionAir have hinted they might be looking for presenters with a "fresh, new image", and let's face it, my other career strand, my writing, seems to have stalled. I just don't think the world is ready for my talent.'

'This cryogenic thing seems an extreme reaction though. How is it going to help?'

'For one thing I think it will keep my audience engaged and pique new interest. Sales of my books could go through the roof. It'll be like when a famous artist or writer dies, people will belatedly recognise me as a creative genius. Like Van Gogh or Franz Kafka, I will be feted once the world is deprived of my presence.'

'Mmm, think maybe you should lay off the gin. I hate to say it, but it could be that you'll be completely forgotten when you're no longer around.'

'Well, don't forget the publicity that's going to be generated. Once I'm frozen, Nella's going to send a pre-recorded statement to VisionAir for transmission. Great publicity. Means I got a very good deal.'

'Now I did wonder about that. These things don't come cheap. Anyway, what do the various women in your life think about the idea?'

'Well, Lanae and her cousin don't actually know yet. They will of course once the interview goes out. I expect they'll be distraught, and fur may well fly when Lanae finds out about my relationship with her cousin, but by the time I'm thawed out I'm sure they'll have moved on.'

'And what about your other young, er, friend?'

'Nella? It was her that gave me the idea. She works in the Cryopreservation Unit. She told me about the reduced length process and brokered the deal. I think she rather likes the notion of preserving me until she catches up, so to speak. Anyway, it gives her the opportunity to get career and motherhood and all the other malarky out of her system.'

'So, you think you and she will make a go of it in 2099?'

'Depends if she's kept her looks, I suppose. I may well have my pick of young, nubile females by then, especially with my assured celebrity status.'

'Well, good luck. I just hope all turns out well for you,' I'd said.

Suddenly I'd felt really sad, Codie. I know he can be a bit of a zonker, but Zane is the only one of my buddies I've known since I was a youngster. I was going to miss the guy. I'd reached out and pulled him into a hug and he'd hugged me back quite tightly. When we'd drawn apart, I'd thought I could see tears in those famous turquoise eyes. I'd always suspected he's not as tough as he'd like to make out. On impulse, I'd asked, 'You going by yourself to this what's it called?'

'Cryopreservation Unit, yes, I was . . .' he'd

looked at me hopefully. So, of course, I'd suggested going along. I was quite intrigued to see what he'd let himself in for, and still thought maybe I could persuade him to change his mind.

Well, Codie, when we got to the place this morning it looked rather bleak and deserted. It's set slightly apart from the Midtown Zone Medical Facilities and occupies a separate block. A bland two-storey building with very few windows, very uninviting I thought.

'You sure about this?' I'd asked Zane. 'Not too late to change your mind you know.'

Zane had just ignored me and strode manfully on towards the entrance. Once past the Entrypoint Retinal Scanner, we entered a completely empty waiting area but after a moment or two a beautiful girl arrived behind the reception desk. She was slender and exotic-looking, with a pale, luminous complexion and shiny black hair coiled on top of her head. I guessed she must be Nella because as soon as he saw her old Zaney went into suave, urbane mode, walking over to the desk and kissing her hand. I thought how different she was to Lanae who is blonde, curvy, and vivacious. She's also beautiful but in a slightly vacuous, artificial way. Nella seemed to ooze serenity and calm and didn't react like a lot of females do around Zane, playing with their hair and becoming over-animated. She'd looked at him quite coldly I'd thought. Don't think he'd noticed. He was too busy checking he'd been allocated the Enhanced Luxury Package. We never got to see a doctor or consultant or anything which at the time I'd thought a bit odd.

Anyway, once Nella was on the scene I was more or less dismissed. But just as I was about to slope off, Nella whispered that she'd like to have a quick word once she'd got Zane settled and asked me to have a seat in the waiting area. I couldn't imagine why but thought perhaps it was to offer some sort of pastoral support to accompanying friends and relatives.

She'd left the door to the Enhanced Luxury Package room slightly open, and you know me, you always said I was a nosey noodle, and it was such a bizarre situation to be sending off your oldest mate to some sort of cryogenic limbo that I couldn't resist popping in my acoustic zingers and having a listen in.

'Here you go, Zaney,' I heard Nella say, and there was a clunking sound as she presumably placed a glass on his bedside table. 'I'm gonna miss you, baby,' I'd heard her whisper.

'Just think Nella, come 2099, you'll be an experienced woman of 43 and I'll still be 42. Just ripe for being your sweet toy boy. How about you slip out of that uniform and into this bed for a few minutes? I can give you something to keep you going for the next 15 years.' *Typical Zane*, I'd thought, *never misses an opportunity.*

I'd heard Nella laugh. 'Unfortunately, I'm going to have to refuse that delightful offer. Unlike some folks, I need to work. I definitely can't afford to lose this job.'

'Ah shame,' I'd heard Zane say. 'For me, the next 15 years are going to pass in a trice. Never mind, you can concentrate on your career, maybe have a couple of kids, until the man of your dreams re-enters your life.' I heard him slurping his drink. 'Now you better leave before you give into temptation.'

Nella came out as I was pulling the zingers out of my ears. I'd been puzzled by the look on her face. It was almost contemptuous, totally at odds with the way she had spoken to Zane a moment before. She'd sighed and gestured for me to come over to the reception desk.

'Corban isn't it?' she'd asked. 'Good friend of Zane's, are you?'

'Yeah, well we go way back. He's OK once you get to know him.'

Nella had shaken her head. 'Corban, this isn't as it seems and definitely not what Zane is expecting.' She must have seen my alarm because she'd placed a hand on my arm and continued. 'I can't go into it all now; it wouldn't be appropriate. But let's just say that although Zane isn't actually going to come to any physical harm, he is in for a shock, and I'd feel happier if he had some support. Zoot knows why, but there it is.' She'd looked down at the TimeSpot on her wrist. 'Can you come back in three hours, at about 1500 hours?'

I'd nodded and she'd looked relieved. 'Now with the Sleeptite I've given him he'll be out for the count in a few moments, but don't worry, by the time you return I can promise he'll be back in the land of the living.'

I'd been about to ask for more details, I was feeling I should demand them on Zane's behalf, but abruptly Nella had turned her back and walked away. From an overhead speaker an automated voice instructed me to "leave the building immediately" and a screen came down blocking the reception desk from view. This was followed by a loud, dissonant buzzing noise which had the desired effect of encouraging me to make a speedy exit.

Totally confused, I'd made my way to the nearest bar to consider my options. I'd wondered whether Zane might be involved in some sort of reality broadcast for VisionAir or if he was to be kidnapped and tortured for information. Had he somehow got himself involved with political espionage? However, If there was anything sinister going on, it didn't make sense that Nella had asked me to return. As I'd calmed my nerves with a double vodka, I contemplated contacting the authorities but doubted I would get a positive response. In the end I decided that the most logical course of action was to return to the unit at 1500 hours and see what transpired then. For some inexplicable reason, I'd actually trusted Nella when she'd said that Zane would come to no harm. What would you have done, I wonder, Codie?

Anyway, I was back at the unit at the appointed

hour and mightily relieved when, on my arrival, the entrance door swung open revealing old Zaney slumped on a settee in the reception area. He was wearing a baseball cap pulled low down on his forehead, which seemed incongruent with his expensive jeans and cashmere sweater. As I'd approached, I could see that his face was very flushed.

'Corban, Corban, man am I glad to see you. Get me out of here.' He was trembling and his speech was slightly slurred.

The next moment Nella had joined us. 'He's fine,' she'd assured me. 'He's a little bit woozy still, but fine.' She'd turned to Zane. 'I don't think we'll be seeing each other again, Zane. But despite everything I do hope things work out for you in the future. Oh, by the way, the baseball cap's on me.'

I'd pulled Zane to his feet, and we'd made it out of the building and onto the next transporter back to his apartment. After two strong coffees he'd told me of his rude awakening.

As he'd regained consciousness, it seemed to Zane that only a few moments had passed and, glancing around the room, he was surprised that it looked exactly the same as it had pre-cryopreservation. Then Nella had entered the room, and she too appeared totally unchanged. As Zane had been exclaiming over her youthful appearance, he had experienced a nasty shock as Lanae and Rosa had emerged at the foot of his bed.

He had attempted to compliment them as they too seemed not to have aged, but they were not to be charmed and apparently their response had been hostile. Lanae had said that she could hardly bear to look at him, and Rosa had said, 'Just wait until you look beneath the sheets, Zane.'

At this Zane had begun to panic and begged Nella to tell him what had been done to him.

'Corban, I was terrified. Those two witches were cackling with glee and Nella, well, she just looked uncomfortable. I was dreading what she was going to tell me.'

'So, Zane, come on, mate. Tell me,' I'd said impatiently. I was very relieved that Zane was alive, unfrozen, and appeared to be in one piece, but still felt bad about leaving him in the hands of three vindictive women.

'Well, before Nella could say anything Lanae really put the boot in. I was petrified when she said, "So Zane as you may or may not have guessed you have not actually undergone cryopreservation. This is why the three of us still look so young and beautiful. You've only been out of it for a few hours not 15 years, but it's been long enough for you to undergo other procedures." I mean, for Zoot's sake, who wouldn't be terrified? I asked her what she was talking about. That I couldn't believe that anything terrible would have taken place in a medical facility. And do you know what she said, Corban?'

I'd shaken my head.

'She s-aid,' he stuttered. 'She said, "Zane, you obviously don't realise how unpopular you are. Even the medical professionals had no qualms in assisting in your, er, modifications. Let's just say you're not quite the man you used to be." Well obviously, I really lost it then and Nella, bless her, took pity on me.'

I'd smiled in encouragement. 'So, what did she tell you, Zane?' I'd asked.

'She said, "Zane, calm down. Nothing has happened to your manhood, but we have given you a little something to remember us by." And well, this is it.' Zane pulled off the baseball cap and swept his blond-streaked hair back from his forehead.

I'd stared at the black smudgy mess in confusion. Then, leaning forward I could see the remains of a word, "RAT".

'I couldn't make it out at first,' said Zane. 'That's because I was looking in the mirror that Nella had passed me. The word looked like "TAR" but with a backwards "R". Then I realised that it was distorted by the mirror and actually said "RAT" but what really spooked me was I thought they'd tattooed it on. Anyway, once the vicious bitches saw I'd got the message they left and then Nella put me out of my misery. It's black marker pen apparently so it will come off completely in time. She's rubbed a bit off to show me, but I need to carry on rubbing it with nail varnish remover. She wouldn't let me stay and remove it properly. She'd only got use of the room and reception area for a few hours. Called in a few favours to teach me a lesson she said.' He'd sniffed and looked down. 'Suppose I deserve it,' he said, lifting his head and looking at me to gauge my reaction.

'Well, you had been stringing them all along and without any respect for their feelings. I'm mightily relieved though that they didn't inflict any permanent damage. How did they all find out about your various infidelities?'

'Hmm, well, I suppose I was running a big risk with Lanae and Rosa. I didn't think they saw that much of each other nowadays and I'd indicated to Rosa that me and Lanae were breaking up. That was sort of true. I was going to break up with her, but I was actually going to break up with both of them and you know I thought I'd be out of the firing line whilst frozen and then that I'd be free to make a go of it with Nella or someone equally as lovely when I came round.'

'What about Nella? How did she find out? I'd asked. 'She saw me in a restaurant with Lanae. Then did some digging I suppose and realised she was one of three women in my life. Can't believe she plotted and planned all this with them though.'

'Yes, what I don't get is how she managed to convince you of this special deal if you didn't see any specialists or consultants or anyone.'

'Corban, I did. Or to be precise, I thought I did but turns out Nella has a brother who's an actor and he has a couple of mates who thought they'd like to help him teach a lesson to the cad who broke his little sister's heart.'

'You know Zane, you can't blame them. I'd feel the same if someone had deceived Codie like that,' I'd said.

'Yes, she was a lovely little lass,' Zane had said, sighing.

'She had a soft spot for you when she was young, but all the girls did, Zane, and you weren't always kind to them.'

'Yes, I do feel a bit bad about that sometimes,' said Zane, as he'd ruffled his hair over his forehead and replaced the baseball cap. 'Corban, could you get some nail varnish remover from your wife do you think?'

'I can,' I'd said, 'but it will have to wait until tomorrow. It's my sister's birthday today and I always take her a bouquet of white roses. So, I better get off. You going to be alright?'

'Yeah, 'course mate. I'm sorry for holding you up and thanks for everything. I've been a bit of a zickster, haven't I? Anyway, I better get this lot put away.' He indicated a pile of miscellaneous items occupying a corner of the room. 'Nella said she was going to get them put into storage for me, but obviously that's not going to happen now.'

'Quite a collection, you've got there.' I'd walked over to the pile, picking through some trophies, certificates, copies of Zane's various publications, and a few holographic photograph cubes, the sort that were so popular in the late 2050s. Then something weird happened. I saw you. Well, obviously not you literally but a holophoto cube showing you as a teenager performing a pirouette. If was a graceful, beautiful image. You were dressed in a lilac and silver leotard, twirling on pointe in your satin ballet shoes, your dark red hair drawn high into a bun. I remembered how often you had practised that movement to achieve the perfect spin. You had a real passion and talent for ballet when you were 15 years old.

'Zane, how in Zoot's name did you get this holophoto of Codie?' I'd asked.

Zane had peered at the cube. 'Oh, hadn't realised it was Codie. Was when I first started with VisionAir, I think. Went along to cover a dancing competition. It just struck me as exquisite. The photographer had truly captured a young girl's joy in her achievement. A perfect moment frozen in time.'

I'd been surprised by that. As I'd left, I'd grasped his arm. 'You know, Zane, you should embrace your sensitive side more often, it suits you,' I'd told him.

So, Codie, that's the story. I'm hoping it has a positive outcome for Zane and he begins to live his life in a less superficial way. Anyway, he's let me keep the holophoto cube, so now I've got a reminder of how you looked at your most beautiful before addiction and illness took its toll. I won't leave the cube here though; it might get damaged. Although you've got one of the best plots in the crematorium, it's a bit exposed to the elements. I'm putting your birthday roses just beneath your memorial plaque, and I'm hoping to dream of your perfect pirouette tonight.

# CLOSE TO THE EDGE

Zinnia was just about to enter the shed when she heard Geoff crying. She had never heard him crying noisily before. When he had shed tears it had been very occasionally and very quietly on the birth of their children and the death of his father. This loud, spluttering sobbing sound was something entirely new. She had been about to ask him what he wanted for lunch, but it seemed insensitive to disturb such distress. She walked quietly away and back into the house.

When Geoff appeared about 15 minutes later, he was quite bright and cheery.

'What's for lunch my darling?' he asked. 'I quite fancy a cheese and pickle sandwich.'

They ate their sandwiches whilst going through the morning's post, as was their custom, and Geoff said he would take his cup of tea down to the shed as he wanted to 'get back to sorting some more stuff out.'

Zinnia was perplexed. She was relieved that he now seemed happy enough but how strange that he had so quickly recovered from the unusual and rather dramatic episode of grief. She decided to ring her daughter, Giselle, to see if she could shed any light on the matter.

'Giselle how did Dad seem last time you spoke to

him?' she asked her daughter.

'Same as ever,' said Giselle. 'You know Dad, man of few words. Why do you ask?'

Her mother explained what she had overheard. Giselle was amazed. 'How weird. Why don't you just ask him.'

'Because, my darling daughter, your father is a very private man and he hates it when anyone pries into his affairs as unfortunately your grannie has done all of his life. No, if he wants me to know what the problem is, I am sure he will tell me.'

Nevertheless, Zinnia could not stop worrying. Later that day she walked into the bedroom to find Geoff standing in front of the mirror, pulling faces. He turned around quickly and rather guiltily when he realised, she had entered the room.

'Oh, hello, darling,' he said. 'Thought I could see a spot, but it must have been a trick of the light.'

The next day Zinnia had arranged to meet her friend Margaret for coffee. She was a little anxious about leaving Geoff alone, but he seemed his usual cheerful self and she knew it was good for them to spend some time apart meeting their own friends and pursuing individual interests now that they were retired. She didn't mention her fears to her friend but decided to catch an earlier bus back home instead of looking around the shops as she would normally have done. As she entered the house, she could hear Geoff talking to someone. No not talking, shouting really.

'It's all got too much,' he yelled. 'I just can't go on

anymore.'

Zinnia closed the front door loudly so that he would think she had just got in. She walked into the lounge where Geoff was standing quite alone holding a sheaf of papers. His face was rather flushed.

'Hello, Zinny, you're early,' he said smiling. Now seeming completely calm.

'Yes, it was a bit hectic in town,' said Zinnia. 'I didn't feel like shopping today.'

They passed a pleasant afternoon going through some old family photographs which they were planning to scan into the computer. Geoff appeared happy and relaxed. Zinnia decided to do nothing until she had spoken to their son Patrick who was due to visit in a couple of days' time.

Patrick had rung his mother to ask if it would be all right to bring Emily along for lunch. She had said that it would be absolutely fine but that there was just something she could do with some advice on at some point during his visit that needed to be discussed privately. He was intrigued and asked if she would give him some clue, but she said that it was possibly something better discussed face-to-face.

During the 45-minute car journey he gave Emily a potted history of his parents.

'You'll get on great with my folks,' he enthused. 'They are very different to each other but make a lovely couple. Mum was brought up in a big family. She was one of six. She has two sisters and three brothers. Her parents were very easy-going and supportive and as a result she's outgoing, confident and optimistic. All three girls in the family were given names beginning with "Z". Mum is Zinnia and I have an Aunt Zita and an Aunt Zena.'

'Wow, Zinnia's a great name,' said Emily. 'I wish I had an unusual name like that. It's much more memorable than Emily.'

Patrick patted her knee. 'Well just like you, Emily is a lovely name,' he reassured her. 'Then Dad is Geoff,' he went on. 'He's totally opposite to Mum in personality. He was an only child and, to be honest, didn't have a very happy childhood. Mum never speaks ill of anyone but even she says that Grannie is meddlesome. She is and she's also very self-centred and a bit spiteful. I don't think that either she or Grandad really wanted children. She likes to have her own way and my Dad has always had a mind of his own, so it was a bit uncomfortable for him growing up. Mum says that she thinks living in that environment affected his confidence. Anyway he's a clever man and when he met Mum he really blossomed and went on to have his own accountancy business which was very successful but he and Mum decided that they wanted to spend a bit more time together so he sold the business at the end of last year.'

'Are they happy now?' asked Emily. 'I know my Dad found it difficult when he retired.'

'Well they are very happy together,' said Patrick, 'but Dad spent so much time at work that I think at

SUZI HAYWARD

the moment he is still "finding his feet" a bit. Mum had worked part-time for years and built up a big circle of friends so it's not so different for her, but I think he's still at the stage where he's considering options re voluntary work and clubs and so on.'

The couple were given a warm welcome by Zinnia and Geoff and lunch was very pleasant. Towards the end of the meal, Zinnia asked if Emily had visited the area before.

'Yes,' said Emily. 'As a matter of fact I have a friend who lives quite close to here and I'm going to be coming over on a regular basis for the next few weeks because I'm giving her a hand with a project she's got involved with.'

Zinnia was interested to hear this. She had taken to Emily and very much hoped to see her again.

'Ooh, that sounds exciting, can you talk about it?' she asked.

'Well, it is very interesting actually,' Emily said. 'Kirsty, my friend from college, moved here when she got married and is on extended maternity leave at the moment. Like me, one of her specialisms is drama and she's got involved with the Totbury Players. They're putting on a fairly ambitious production in a few months and Kirsty's helping out with auditions over the next few weeks. They've had loads of interest from potential actors and she's asked me to give her a hand with casting. We're casting for the two main leads next week.'

'What play is it?' asked Zinnia.

'It's called *Close to The Edge*. It's about a man who becomes suicidal after losing his family and job.'

'Sounds a bit grim, doesn't it?' said Zinnia.

She glanced across at Geoff, trying to encourage him to join the conversation but strangely he just looked down at his plate and mumbled, 'Yes.' He seemed to be pushing his pudding around the plate without much enthusiasm which was disappointing because she had made the lemon meringue as it was one of his favourites.

'Anyway it's not all "doom and gloom",' continued Emily. 'It does have its lighter moments but I won't spoil the story for you in case you decide to come and see it.'

Zinnia remembered that she needed to have a word with Patrick and asked him to help her wash up. She suggested that Geoff show Emily some of the photos they had been sorting out but strangely he seemed reluctant to do so and sprang up, saying, 'No, no. I insist on doing the washing up. You've given us such a wonderful meal. You three look at the photos and I'll bring you all coffee in a few minutes.'

So, Patrick and Emily left before the opportunity arose for the "quiet word". Never mind, Zinnia decided; she'd pop over and see her son sometime soon and also take the opportunity to tell him what a lovely girl Emily was.

The following week Geoff stood nervously at the side of the stage waiting for his turn. He had always dreamt of becoming an actor and almost auditioned for a school play, but he had made the mistake of telling his mother of his intention. Her response had been a crushing blow.

'To be an actor you need confidence and charisma, my darling. You're much too shy. You'll stumble over your words and go red and look foolish. Better stick to the things you're good at.'

Well he was telling no-one on this occasion. He'd practised the audition piece so many times he barely needed a script. He walked out onto the stage with all the confidence he could muster.

'It's all got too much,' he yelled. 'I just can't go on anymore.'

Emily was amazed. Who knew that Patrick's Dad was such a wonderful actor? He was even managing to cry real tears. He made the other auditionees look like complete amateurs. She looked around at the rest of the casting panel. They were nodding and beaming. *Close to the Edge* was going to be a massive success.

# THE RIGHT FOOT

Forty years. It's a long time and should be celebrated. Especially as Claire and I have had such a wonderful marriage. I guess it's because we're not just suited physically but also intellectually. I think that's where many marriages go wrong. They don't seem to endure as people age. For us, being good friends as well as fantastic lovers is important, as is honesty. We don't lie to each other but, having said that, there is just one thing I've never told Claire the whole truth about.

You know I reckon if I'd spoken about it much earlier in our relationship, she would have been OK, and we'd have had a good laugh and then maybe brought it up as a sort of "in-joke" from time to time. I didn't though and I don't think I can now because for Claire that first evening was magical and wonderful. If she were to find out the truth after all these years, it would shake her self-belief no end and even add an edge of deceit to our relationship. The only problem is that there is someone else who knows the truth. Someone who up until now hasn't caused any problems because he hasn't been around. Who knew he would come back after all these years?

* * *

Claire was delighted when she found out the identity of her best-friend's new guy. 'Marty, you'll never guess who Jenny's seeing?' She was actually hopping about with excitement.

'No, lay it on me one time,' I responded in my usual laid-back manner.

To be fair, I was quite interested because since she divorced boring Bruce, Jenny's online dating exploits have been a good source of entertainment. Me and Claire have a pretty young outlook on life even though we're well into our sixties. We still do daft things, dafter since our retirement. It might be because we're childless and don't have to behave like responsible adults all the time. Anyway, Jenny seems to be enjoying a new lease of life, and she makes a very welcome change to our more staid friends whose conversation largely centres around their gardens and grandchildren.

'Baz, Baz Thorpe.' Claire flopped down on the settee next to me. 'You used to hang around with him at school, didn't you?'

'But he's been in Australia for the last fifty years or so.'

'Well, he's back now and it looks like he and Jenny may become an item. So, I've told her to bring him along to the party.'

'Oh, right, cool,' I said, although I was feeling anything but.

'Well, you don't seem very excited.'

Claire looked disappointed and I could sort of

understand why. Yeah, back in the day Baz had been my best mate but it was a big relief when he emigrated. Quite simply he knew too much.

'We *were* good mates, but we lost touch and I don't think there'll be much common ground now.' I tried to justify my lack of enthusiasm.

'I don't know so much,' Claire squeezed my knee. 'He still loves his sixties music apparently.' She began to sing a "mash up" of some of our old favourites.

I suggested she have a nice long bath whilst I got the supper. I wanted time by myself to think things through. I poured Claire a giant glass of wine.

'Go on, relax.' I shooed her out of the room. Safely ensconced in the kitchen, chopping garlic and onions, I thought back to that fateful day.

\* \* \*

It was approaching Christmas time 1968 when I was fourteen, and as was the custom, the Joseph Baker Memorial School were laying on early evening parties for their students. Overall, the teachers were a good bunch and didn't mind too much giving up their free time to bring a bit of joy to the kids in our grim northern town. We thought we'd struck it lucky when Mrs Joyce and Mr Blenkinsop were tasked with organising the third-year bash. Mrs Joyce was friendly and easy-going, and Mr Blenkinsop was ex-Army, a bit strict but fair and generally well liked by most of the school. As usual the lads and lasses had formed separate huddles. Mr Blenkinsop was having none of it.

'Right, it's about time that you lads learnt how to accompany a lady on a social occasion. All these young ladies are looking lovely, and they deserve a polite and attentive companion. Now the way we're going to pair up is, I'm going to ask each young lady to remove her right shoe and put it in a pile on the floor. We're going to have a nice tune and I'm going to ask the lads to jog round the shoes and when the music stops to pick one and whoever the shoe belongs to will be your partner for the evening. OK lads?'

The "lads" had managed to nod; they weren't that enthused by the idea. The girls had giggled but begun to remove their shoes. Me, I saw a major opportunity. I'd fancied Gillian Fletcher ever since I first saw her. She was well fit, slim, blonde, confident, the best-looking girl in school. I'd dreamt of finding the courage to strike up a conversation with her. Now here was my chance. I didn't know that much about lasses' footwear, but I studied her left foot. She was wearing a black patent slip-on with a little bow on the front. I was getting that shoe. The music started up. It was one of my favourites, but I didn't start dancing and get side-tracked. I kept focussed. When the music stopped, I lunged for the shoe and got it, almost pushing Keith Brewster to the floor. Mr Blenkinsop had frowned but let it go. He issued further instructions.

'Right lads now you've each got a shoe, it's your job to find out which young lady it fits. You have five minutes.'

I started out determinedly towards Gillian Fletcher but before I reached her, I saw that nerd Nigel Parker was already at her side. I looked at the shoe she had just returned to her right foot. It looked the same as the one I held in my hand. I looked frantically around. Most of the girls were now in possession of both shoes and their evening's partner but, oh no, Claire Midgley was still standing with an unshod right foot and glancing around uncertainly. Then horror-struck I examined her left foot. She was wearing the same shoes as Gillian Fletcher. I hadn't reckoned on there being two identical pairs. Trust me. Now I was stuck with Claire, the most timid girl in the third year. What a boring evening lay ahead. I glanced over at my mate Baz who was laughing as he helped Big Tilly (a large but friendly lass) on with her shoe. He wasn't really bothered about anything because he was emigrating with his parents to Australia in a few days' time and that was all he could think about.

Claire was turned away at that moment and I took the opportunity to mouth, 'fuck,' whilst pointing the shoe in her direction. 'Shit,' Baz mouthed back. Then he took Tilly's hand and led her away, leaving me to my fate. He couldn't give a toss. All that he was thinking about was that he would soon be well in with all the beach babes in

Oz.

So, there was nothing for it. I'd had to "man up". I really didn't want to get on the wrong side of old Blenkinsop. I walked over to Claire and did my best Prince Charming impression. It was weird though; the minute I held her hand my feelings began to change. Her hand was so small and soft; I felt protective somehow.

Once we were seated in the hall, she thanked me really nicely. It was strange for a lad of fourteen, but I was impressed by how ladylike she was – gentle and softly-spoken. For the first time ever, I actually looked properly at her face. If I'm honest, I'd been a bit put off by the specs (pink plastic – the free ones on the NHS in those days), but I saw that behind the lens her eyes were quite lovely, a most unusual shade of green. She'd put on a bit of eyeliner and some sort of sparkly stuff on her eyelids, and that got to me. I imagined her, nervous and excited, preparing for the party; maybe hoping the unfamiliar makeup would inject a bit of magic into the event. At that moment I really wanted the evening to be special for her.

I smiled. 'You look nice,' I said.

She turned her head slightly and her shampoo smelt lovely, fresh, and clean with some sort of an apple fragrance going on. She had nice if unfashionable hair – a bit curly, shoulder-length; the colour almost reminded me of our cat, Toff (named for the toffee colour of his coat). Claire smiled back and suddenly she looked pretty.

'I like your shirt, the colour really suits you,' she said. I stuttered my thanks. I was proud of the shirt. It was blue and new, with a modern pointy collar – one of the few items of clothing I possessed which was neither school uniform nor sports kit. My mum had allowed me to choose it as an early "Christmas Box" and if I squinted in the mirror the right way, I fancied it made my eyes look the same colour as Steve McQueen's – I'd recently seen *Bullitt* at the Odeon.

It was nice talking to Claire, it didn't feel confrontational or awkward as it did with some of the other girls in school. There was no pouting or giggling going on. I liked that. Before long we were laughing and chatting as though we'd been friends for ages. When the dancing started, we moved easily and confidently together.

'I love this group.' Claire had said as we gyrated to the Rolling Stones. 'I'm getting their latest LP for Christmas.'

I hadn't had her pegged as a Stones fan, but I was beginning to realise she had hidden depths and obviously great taste in music, and the girl could move. I remember looking across the room and noticing that Gillian Fletcher was not dancing or even talking to nerdy Nigel but chatting with her friends. Whilst I was having a brilliant evening and basically everything was groovy.

* * *

I'd not been looking forward to losing my mate Baz, but after the party I felt relieved that he was going away. He'd been the only one who knew I'd been besotted with Gillian Fletcher, and he couldn't believe it when I told him what a great evening I'd had with Claire or that I wanted to see her again. Initially, he thought I'd been joking.

'Yeah, yeah,' he'd said and then made a vaguely obscene remark at Claire's expense. I'd wanted to hit him, but I'd felt embarrassed and, if I'm honest a bit scared, he was bigger and stronger than me. I'd walked away but felt an uneasy sense of betrayal – I'd let Claire down when my gut instinct was to respect and care for her.

I went round to see Baz on the morning of his departure and said all the right things, but my heart wasn't in it. I was relieved he didn't mention Claire and when he and I lost touch after a couple of letters I thought it was for the best. If that idiot had been around, he would have blurted out something hurtful to Claire and spoilt our friendship which had blossomed when I'd asked her to meet me in town a few days after the party.

I really liked being with Claire. We saw a lot of each other over the next few years and I think the relationship was good for both of us. She brought out my serious side – I began to read more literature and started to compose poetry. Much to the surprise of teachers and my parents I even got good exam results. Claire became more extrovert and confident. She told me later that I did wonders for her self-esteem because I complimented her on her appearance which apparently no-one else had bothered to do. We had dated other people for a while when we'd left school and moved on to higher education out of our local area, but we'd always kept in touch and got together again in our early twenties. We'd been married for over forty years, and I always blessed the day I'd picked her shoe from the pile on the floor.

* * *

Now Baz's reappearance has cast a blight on our 40th Wedding Anniversary party. I imagine a sixty something version of his tactless, boisterous fourteen-year-old self and shudder. It might seem ridiculous that a few insensitive remarks can threaten mine and Claire's long and strong relationship, but I love her so much and want our celebrations to be perfect. There's nothing to be done though, the invitations have already been issued, the party is next week. I just hope and pray that Baz has mellowed and gained some discretion and charm.

* * *

So here we are, all togged up nicely and almost ready to receive our guests. Claire looks wonderful. She doesn't look anything like her age. No glasses now either. A few years back she had corrective surgery for her cataracts and severe myopia. Her green eyes really sparkle, and she's wearing a wonderful emerald silk dress which skims over her still trim figure and finishes just above her slim ankles. Black patent shoes as well which, of course, her younger sister Debbie spots right away. She's arrived early to help with the preparations and generally get in the way.

'Hey Claire, like the shoes. Mmm, black patent. Hoping to re-create your Cinderella moment?' Debbie gives me a sly look.

'Well, they're a lot more expensive and I'm happy to say much more comfortable than those I was wearing when me and Marty got together.' Claire squeezes my arm. She laughs. 'I only got those horrible things because Gillian Fletcher had a pair and I think I hoped they'd give me some of her sex appeal. She was a bit of a boy magnet.' She looks directly at me. 'But, I have a lot to thank those shoes for.' She leans forward and kisses me briefly on the lips.

Debbie guffaws as she alternately arranges and eats the prawn vol-au-vents. 'You've got to be kidding. Sex appeal? Have you seen the size of her recently?'

'Debs, don't be so unkind.' Claire nudges her sister. 'I don't think she has an easy time of it now, and I agree that she has let herself go a bit, but back in 1968 she was every boy's dream date, isn't that right Marty?'

'Well, you know what most young men are like, very little taste and absolutely no sense.' I wrap my arms firmly round Claire. There's only a select few who've got the nous to recognise true beauty and intelligence.' I whisper in her ear, 'You're looking gorgeous tonight. I can't wait for the party to be over.'

Which is true and definitely not because I'm scared of anything Baz or anyone else might say. Nothing and no-one can threaten our marriage, which I now realise is rock-solid with foundations built on love and knowledge, not flimsy fantasy. What a conceited sod I've been to imagine that a woman like Claire would be traumatised by a silly school-boy's infatuations and how lucky I am to have her love even though she so clearly perceives my soppy self-absorption. I lean in to kiss her again taking the opportunity to slip a diamond and ruby eternity ring out of my jacket pocket and onto her finger. 'Here's to another wonderful forty years,' I say.

# THE VISIT

It was two days before Wendy plucked up the courage to read the letter. Her mother's writing was immediately recognisable, and it was seldom that her correspondence contained anything to lift the spirits. Wendy felt sure that there would be several pages of complaints, and that her own shortcomings would be amply dwelt upon. However, at the same time, she did feel a bit guilty. Although her mother was often unreasonable and unkind, she was elderly, frail and increasingly lonely. It would shortly be the third anniversary of Wendy's father's death and she knew that a visit to her mother could and should not be avoided at this time.

Eventually, after downing half a glass of red wine, she tore the envelope open. Her heart sank when she saw that the letter was several pages long and written in red ink – this never boded well. She scanned it quickly. It appeared that Mum was very hurt that Wendy had not visited recently, that she had fallen out with her best friend at the sheltered housing complex, had  made an official complaint against the manager, and had decided to look for alternative accommodation. This was not good news. Wendy doubted that her mother would survive another move and she felt it unlikely that she would find somewhere that offered more congenial surroundings than Latimer House. She knew she must do her best to dissuade Mum from this course of action. So, she picked up the phone and made arrangements to visit at the weekend.

* * *

Wendy dressed carefully for the visit. Her mother, Molly Durham, had previously owned a dress shop, Molly's Modes, and liked to critique Wendy's clothes and appearance. She knew that in her mother's opinion she was overweight, and that Molly attributed this to Wendy's lack of self-discipline with regard to diet and alcohol consumption. Apart from Sanatogen Wine, Molly had rarely been known to consume any alcoholic beverage and now had little interest in food.

Reluctant to arrive empty-handed, Wendy had bought her mother some magazines, a large pack of notelets and a book of postage stamps. It was difficult to know what to take. Confectionary was not usually appreciated, and Molly declared herself allergic to any products which were perfumed, so luxury toiletries and cosmetics were completely out of the question. However, she did write several letters a day – to friends, acquaintances, magazines and anyone she came into contact with who she felt would benefit from her wisdom and advice.

It seemed very quiet in the building and Wendy

did not see any of the staff or other residents as she entered. She had keys for the front door and her mother's room. She went up the stairs and along the corridor. Although she had a key, Wendy always knocked first and waited for a response; but this time there was no answer. She thought perhaps her mother was in the ensuite shower room. Knocking again, she turned the handle and the door swung open. She entered, calling out, 'It's only me, Mum,' as she did so.

At first, she thought the room to be empty but then became aware that someone was sitting in the armchair near the window; someone very small. Wendy crossed the room and saw a young girl. She appeared to be deeply distressed and was sobbing noisily into a white, lace-trimmed handkerchief. Wendy knelt down in front of her.

'Hello,' she said. 'Do you know where Mrs Durham is?'

The child did not respond – just looked at Wendy and then started to cry again. Wendy saw that she was very young, perhaps five or six. She was strangely dressed in an old-fashioned gym slip and white blouse. A pair of plimsolls and grey, knee-length socks completed the outfit. Her small, pale face was surrounded by fine light-brown hair, very badly cut into a bob with an extremely short fringe. Wendy wondered if she was one of the carers' children. Really, was it appropriate to bring them into a place like this? Surely it was not if you were going to leave them unattended in a resident's room. Wendy never felt that she was very good with children. They often seemed a little afraid of her. But she was affected by the child's misery and put out her hand and touched her thin arm.

'What's the matter?' she asked.

'They don't like me anymore,' said the little girl.

'Where is your mother?' asked Wendy.

The little girl looked up at Wendy with pale-blue, red-rimmed eyes. 'No one likes me,' she said, 'not anymore. She said I stole it, but I was going to put it back. I just wanted to put a bit on my hankie. Smell it, it's lovely.' She proffered a rather moist handkerchief.

Reluctantly, Wendy took it and sniffed. A surprisingly rich, smoky scent assailed her nostrils. 'It is nice,' she said, 'What is it?'

'Shali-something,' said the little girl.

'Ah, Shalimar,' said Wendy. She vaguely remembered this had been a favourite perfume of one of her aunts; but she had not come across it for years and it hardly seemed the perfume of choice for a little girl. It was strange but there was something familiar about the child's eyes. Maybe Wendy had met her before; but how odd her clothing was and how unusual to see a young child using a real handkerchief.

'I'm sure they know you only borrowed it,' said Wendy. 'You're a lovely little girl; everyone is bound to like you.' She took a tissue from her bag and wiped the child's tear-stained face.

'Do you like me, Wendy?' said the girl. Wendy was astonished. How did this little girl know her name? But now did not seem the time to question her, she appeared to need reassurance.

'Of course, I do,' she said and gave the child a hug. It crossed her mind that she should possibly not be hugging unknown children but somehow it just seemed appropriate.

'That's all right then. Come on, we have to go now.' The child took Wendy's hand and led her to the door. She was so determined in her grasp and now seemed so much cheered that Wendy hadn't the heart to tell her that she needed to find her mother. They went downstairs and out through the front door. There was a pathway at the side of the building which led to a nice, secluded garden. Another small figure was standing at the end of the path. Wendy saw that this was a little boy, perhaps six or seven years old. He turned and beckoned to the little girl, and she ran over to him immediately. They ran off into the garden together and out of Wendy's sight. There was something unusual about the boy's clothing. Wendy thought that he looked rather like the Just William character of Richmal Crompton's books. He was somewhat dishevelled in appearance and wearing knee-length grey flannel trousers, a white(ish) shirt and a striped tie which was tied rather untidily around his neck. Wendy wondered if both children were dressed for some sort of themed party.

However, she really needed to find her mother as she was apt to become very irritable if kept waiting. Wendy approached the building again. This time she elected to press the intercom. This was answered by one of the staff, Maxine, who said she would be out in a moment.

Seconds later Wendy was greeted by an anxious-looking Maxine, who ushered her into the residents' sitting room.

'Wendy,' she said, 'will you sit down a minute. I've been trying to contact you. I'm afraid that Mum passed away a couple of hours ago; it was very quick, and she didn't suffer. We think she had a heart attack. She died in the ambulance on her way to hospital.'

Wendy felt deeply shocked but also angry and confused. Why had the staff allowed a small child to sit in her dead mother's room? This seemed very disrespectful.

'I have just been up to Mum's room,' she said, 'and there was a little girl sitting there.'

Maxine looked at her in confusion. 'The room has been locked since she left. We haven't had a chance to sort her things out yet.'

'But who was the little girl?' persisted Wendy.

Maxine took her arm. 'Shall we go upstairs together? I realise that you are very upset but really no one has been up there. There are no children here.'

'But I have just been talking to her,' said Wendy. 'She was very upset.'

Maxine led her upstairs and frowned when she found the room unlocked. Wendy explained that she hadn't locked the door on leaving but that it had been open on her arrival. Maxine shook her head, clearly very bewildered. She looked around the room, saying, 'Look, there's no one here, dear.'

'No,' said Wendy. 'She ran off into the garden to join a little boy.'

Maxine led her over to the armchair. 'Sit quietly for a minute; you've had a terrible shock. I can promise you that we won't touch anything in the room for a few days. When you feel up to it you can come back and go through Mum's things.'

Wendy began to cry. 'We didn't part on very good terms. I wish I had visited more often but I always found it so difficult to talk to her. I don't think she ever really liked me. I was a big disappointment to her.'

Maxine looked over at the small bookcase which housed Molly's collection of photograph albums. 'You know I think you may be being a bit hard on yourself. Your Mum was showing me some photographs the other day and she seemed very proud of you.'

\* \* \*

Molly Durham's funeral was quite well attended, and Wendy was pleased to see her Auntie Sheila amongst the mourners. As she was leaving the crematorium, her aunt put an envelope into Wendy's hand.

'Wendy, I found this the other day when I was clearing out some things. I don't think you will have many photos of your mum when she was young. We had very few taken in those days; it was much too expensive. Anyway, I think she was about six years old in this one. I thought you might like it, although I do remember that your Mum was not very happy that day. She had been in trouble for using our Mary's new scent and you know what your Auntie Mary's temper was like.'

Wendy took the photograph from the envelope. It was rather faded; not surprising as it was over eighty years old, but Wendy could quite clearly see a little girl in a gym slip and white blouse, with a badly cut bob and a diffident smile.

'Thank you so much Auntie Sheila,' she said. 'This really means a great deal to me.'

'I thought it would,' said her aunt. 'I know that you will miss her so much. You are so like her in many ways.'

For the first time in her life, Wendy felt that there might be some truth in this. She put the photograph in her handbag alongside the lace-trimmed handkerchief that she had found down the side of Mum's armchair when she had been clearing out her small apartment a few days previously; now freshly laundered but still smelling unmistakably of Shalimar. She walked outside the crematorium to where Molly's family flowers were displayed. 'I miss you, Mum,' she said quietly.

# BRIDGET'S BIG DECISION

'Oh, to be fifteen and a teenager in the swinging sixties,' gushed Mr Murray the supply teacher who was standing in for Jonesy, 4B's usual English teacher who was on sick leave; rumour had it with nervous exhaustion.

Bridget sighed. The Swinging Sixties seemed a long way from Parkfield Secondary Modern which was sited on the edge of the roughest estate in Gainsford and where only the toughest teachers survived. Most of the pupils at Parkfield couldn't wait to leave school at fifteen and start earning some money. Bridget's parents had persuaded her to stay on for the extra year and take her CSEs.

She had only agreed really because her best friend Annie had decided to stay on. Annie had wanted to be a cadet nurse and could only get on the course if she got reasonable exam grades in English and Maths. But then she had started going out with Davie and not been bothered about moving away and being a nurse anymore and then she had said she was leaving and going to start a job in Smileys, the local clothing factory. Apparently, they paid better than the other factories. Everyone was on piece work, and you also got discounted tights and clothing. There was music while you worked and decent food in the canteen. Davie was two years older than Annie, and they were going to save up and get a car and go to some music festivals she said. Once she got her first pay packet, she was going to get a mod haircut and some decent make-up and clothes. Now Bridget had a big decision to make, and it needed to be made that afternoon.

Bridget looked despondently at the empty seat beside her. It was lonely and dull without her best friend. Did she really want to stay on at Parkfield for another year without Annie? And if she felt this way in English, which was by far her favourite subject, how would she feel in Maths and Geography? Bridget shuddered. It didn't bear thinking about. It was a shame because she had been looking forward to this lesson. Mr Murray had asked them all to consider old age and to bring in and read out to the class a poem or piece of writing which they felt best described how it felt to be old. He had said it could be from one of their favourite poets or authors, or something they had written themselves. Not many people knew, but Bridget had been writing poetry for a year or more. She would have felt comfortable reading her own poem with Annie by her side but now it was awkward. She didn't know how it would be received.

Mr Murray had just begun to introduce the topic when there was an unexpected interruption. Mr Trenton, the Headmaster, strode into the classroom accompanied by a couple and a young man about Bridget's own age. He went over to Mr Murray and motioned for him to excuse himself from the class.

'Right, class,' said Mr Murray. 'Just get out *Of Mice & Men* and have a quiet read of that for a few minutes.'

The class dutifully got out the John Steinbeck novel. Some of them read it. Some of them chatted with their neighbour. It was one of the set books for their CSE English exams and not bad but just a shame that it had been "censored" by someone in the school, so a couple of pages were missing. Bridget had tried to get it out of the library to find out what it was they weren't supposed to be reading but it must be popular because it always seemed to be out on loan.

From her seat near the front, Bridget could hear the Head saying to Mr Murray, 'So Christopher will be joining the class next year. Can he sit in for a few minutes whilst I go through some paperwork with his parents?'

The next thing was that Mr Murray was rapping on the desk to attract everyone's attention and Mr Trenton and the couple were leaving the room.

'Listen up you lot. This young gentleman will be joining you next term. His name's Christopher and he's going to be sitting in for the rest of the lesson. Chris, why don't you go and sit next to Bridget. There's a vacant seat there,' he said, motioning to where Annie normally sat.

Bridget turned bright red. Christopher was a

handsome young man. She thought he looked a bit like Stevie Marriott out of The Small Faces. She could not believe he was going to be sitting next to her. He would think she was a right idiot if she read out her poem. But she had nothing else prepared. There was no choice really.

Most of the class hadn't been very imaginative. Mr Murray had introduced the topic a couple of weeks previously and mentioned a few apparently well-known poems, so Shakespeare, T S Eliot, Thomas Hardy and Dylan Thomas appeared to be popular choices. But really Bridget was barely listening. She was overcome with nerves and could hear her heart beating loudly. She thought perhaps she might pass out, but she didn't. Then suddenly it was her turn. She looked down at the sheet in front of her. She didn't need to read from it because she knew the poem off by heart, but holding the piece of paper gave her something to do with her hands. At first her voice seemed to be coming out in a squeak.

'Er, speak up will you please, Bridget,' asked Mr Murray.

Bridget knew that her face was bright red, and some of her classmates appeared to be tittering behind her. But suddenly that spurred her on. What right did they have to laugh at her when most of them didn't even have the guts or creativity to produce their own work? Anyway, what did it matter. She was pretty sure about the decision she was going to make, so why should she care what any of her classmates thought of her? She took a deep breath and began again.

The poem needed to be spoken slowly but strongly. It was about an old person who sat in their room day after day looking at their cherished possessions – things that had once been bright and beautiful but, like them, now appeared old and faded. She had been quite proud of the lines, "She sits all alone in the flowered armchair, Once modern and bright, now dull and threadbare". The elderly person was now lonely and the clock on the mantlepiece marked the hours slowly ticking away towards her death. Bridget's own grandparents were still lively and healthy and didn't really think of themselves as old, in fact they had recently been on their first plane flight to the Isle of Man, but she had based the poem on an old lady who had lived next door. For one reason or another she had no surviving family and few friends. She had died a few years previously, but Bridget remembered visiting her with her mother sometimes. She was always surprised how different the house was inside compared to her own bright welcoming home although the houses looked identical from the outside.

Bridget's poem was just a couple of verses long so that was the good thing about it.

When she had finished reading, Mr Murray said: 'Very nicely read Bridget. It's not one I recognise. Who is the poet? You didn't tell us.'

Bridget was surprised. She had thought it would

have been obvious that it wasn't written by a "real" poet. 'I wrote it,' she replied.

'Bridget, that's very impressive,' said Mr Murray. 'Now who's next, Julian, I think. What have you got for us?'

Julian read a poem that a couple of other students had also picked, and Christopher took the opportunity to lean over and whisper to Bridget, 'You're really talented. That was great.'

Bridget wondered if he was making fun of her, but he was smiling at her sincerely. He really had a lovely face and she thought it was such a shame that the lesson would be over in a few minutes, and he would be gone.

His parents reappeared just before the bell went for the end of class and as he got up to leave, he whispered, 'I'll look forward to seeing you next term.' Bridget didn't like to tell him that this was unlikely.

As she was about to leave the classroom, Mr Murray called over to her, asking if he could have a word.

'Bridget, that was a very good piece of work. Have you written any other poems?' he asked.

Bridget said that she had, and Mr Murray asked her if she would be willing to bring them in as he said he was aware of a National Schools Poetry Competition, and perhaps together they could select one or more of her poems to enter. Bridget was thrilled that someone was interested in her writing. She could not bring herself to tell him that it was unlikely she would be remaining at Parkfield. So, she just agreed to bring them in the following week.

Bridget had arranged to meet Annie at the factory gates when she finished her shift at 4. 30. She'd been so looking forward to meeting her but somehow the big decision didn't seem so clear-cut any more. But maybe all doubts would be gone when she saw her friend again.

Workers were streaming out of the factory gates. A couple of women pushed past Bridget, not bothering to apologise. She saw Annie standing by the gates. She looked smaller than usual, and quite pale and tired.

'You all right, Annie?' Bridget asked.

'Yeah, great, course I am. Couldn't be better and pay day tomorrow.' Her friend managed a smile. 'Now then have you made the decision, cos if you're not interested Mrs Fraser says they'll have to advertise tomorrow.'

'I know you'll think I'm daft, Annie, but do you know, I just don't see me as a machinist, not in the long-term.'

Annie shrugged. 'Well, they don't get that many vacancies and the money's good. Do you really fancy staying at school for another year with no money? I would have thought you'd have been a bit lonely there now. You could start here next week and train alongside me. Still, if you don't fancy it...'

'Annie, I just don't think it's for me really. I

might be making the wrong choice, but I'd love to be able to do something with my writing and maybe if I stay on at school and get some decent exam results, I might just stand a chance. I don't know.'

'OK. I'll tell Mrs Fraser you won't be coming then but make no mistake as soon as it's advertised the job'll be snapped up and you won't get another chance. So, don't blame me when you're miserable by yourself at Parkfield and you've got no money. I was gonna ask you to come out with me and Davie and his mate Steve but I'm thinking now we won't be good enough for you.'

Bridget could see her friend was upset and felt let down, but she just knew if she was being true to herself there was no way she'd be happy working alongside Annie at Smileys, as much as she valued her friendship.

'I'm sorry Annie,' she managed to say. 'I hope that we'll still be friends.'

'We'll see,' muttered Annie, 'but I've got to get home now. I want to wash my hair before Davie comes round.'

She marched off at great speed. Bridget was on the verge of tears but at the same time relieved that she wouldn't be joining the Smiley's workforce the following week.

\* \* \*

Six months later and Bridget seldom saw Annie but was too busy to worry overmuch. She was working hard to get good exam grades and had a Saturday job at the Gainsford Gazette. It turned out that Christopher's uncle was editor there. When he heard of Bridget's success in the National Schools Poetry Competition (although she had not won she had received a certificate for her entry which had been "Highly Commended" and been awarded a place on a day's writing workshop in London) he had been happy to offer her an opportunity and she was to join the Gazette team full-time as a junior reporter after her exams. Her confidence had blossomed, and at the Headmaster's request, she had been happy to read out some of her poems at assembly. In fact, she had achieved some sort of minor celebrity status at Parkfield, especially after her trip to London when she had returned with a brightly coloured mini dress and a geometric haircut.

'You look like Twiggy, only prettier,' Christopher had said when she had taken her place next to him in class. Maybe she was living in the Swinging Sixties after all.

# MASKS

'So, there you go,' the young man pointed to the tins of chopped tomatoes. 'Is there anything else I can help you with today?'

Sadie wished she could think of something else because the young man was by far the nicest and most helpful person she'd talked to all day. She saw that his name was Gerry. Like all the staff in SaveALot, he was wearing a purple and beige overall with a name badge attached to the breast pocket. She couldn't see his mouth because of the now compulsory mask but could tell by his eyes that he was smiling properly and seemed enthusiastic about his role as a supermarket worker. Not all the staff were as keen to help you find something and she wouldn't normally have bothered anyone but recently the supermarket had taken to moving stock around to disguise shortages and it had been a long day.

'No, thank you so much, that's brilliant,' she said, picking up a couple of tins.

'My pleasure,' said Gerry as he strode away.

Sadie finished her shopping and set off home. Unlike most people, she didn't immediately rip off her mask as soon as she left the supermarket. Truth be told, she rather liked wearing a mask and she kept it on until she reached her flat. She had a selection of masks that she had made herself, following some instructions she had found in a magazine. She had selected the material with care, using colours complimentary to her colouring and clothing and enjoyed picking one out each day. She didn't wear them at work because she was an admin assistant at a local firm of solicitors and very seldom had client contact. However, she always wore one on her journey to and from the office because she had to use public transport part of the way. She had even made some for friends and family. Her mother thought it was quite amusing.

'Think you ought to start a cottage industry, Sadie,' she had said to her daughter. 'Might be more fun than working in that stuffy office.'

Sadie didn't mind working in the office. She felt comfortable there and was pleased that she didn't have to encounter too many people during the course of the day. Her mother worried that it wasn't the right environment for a young person. She was always telling Sadie that she ought to be working somewhere where she could mix more with people of her own age.

'Don't you want to get married, Sadie?' she asked on a regular basis. 'Wouldn't you like to have a husband and children and a proper home of your own?'

She didn't seem to consider Sadie's little flat a proper home, but Sadie was rather proud of it. And, yes, she would like to meet someone special and perhaps one day have a family of her own, but it wasn't so easy – not when you had a nose like hers. It had been fine until she had become a teenager but around the age of thirteen or fourteen it just grew and grew and developed an unsightly bump.

'Looks like you've been blessed with your father's nose. Such a shame as you have lovely eyes,' a visiting aunt had said during her biennial visit. Sadie's cousin had stood beside her, a sweet, flaxen-haired girl with a tiny button nose. Around this time Sadie's confidence began to plummet.

Sadie's father was more encouraging. 'You'll grow into it Sadie,' he had said. 'Think of those people who still look great even if their noses are a bit bigger than average, like, er Barbra Streisand.'

Sadie could see that he was struggling to think of attractive female examples, and she wasn't surprised. She guessed that most celebrities with big noses resorted to plastic surgery early on in their careers. But that was not really something she wanted to consider. For one thing, on principle she didn't agree with unnecessary plastic surgery, and for another she really couldn't afford the procedure. Sadie thought it was all right for her father. A big nose didn't look out of place on a big man but, apart from her nose, she was quite petite.

But now, when she was wearing a mask, it seemed that she was on a level playing field with everyone else. She did have attractive dark brown eyes and she made them up to good effect, emphasising them with eyeliner and mascara. As she left her flat each morning, she checked her appearance in the hall mirror and now didn't see a huge nose but a pair of happy and sparkling eyes above a face mask which had been carefully co-ordinated with the rest of her clothing.

A man had given up his seat for her on the bus the previous day and when she had gone into a department store to buy cosmetics an assistant had told her how lucky she was to have such lovely eyes. The young man at the supermarket had been keen to assist her. She wondered how different things would have been if he had seen her without the mask.

The following day she again needed to call into SaveALot. She was glad that she was already wearing her mask as she entered the store as Gerry was greeting customers and handing out hand sanitiser.

'Oh, hello,' he said. 'So nice to see you again.' Somehow, she felt that he didn't say that to all the customers. As she left the store a few minutes later he waved and called out, 'Enjoy your evening.'

There was something in the way that he spoke to her that made her feel special. As she walked home, she told herself not to be so stupid, he was paid to be nice to customers and was obviously just very good at his job. But she couldn't stop thinking about him. She thought he was very attractive with his dark blonde hair and twinkly hazel eyes. He looked as though he spent quite a lot of time outdoors as his skin was sun-tanned and he had an athletic build. He definitely wouldn't be interested in her if he saw her without the mask. She could imagine that he could have his pick of any number of pretty girls. Why would he choose her?

A couple of days later she remembered that it was her Aunt Suzi's birthday at the weekend. She knew what she would get her. Aunt Suzi didn't download her music like most people nowadays. She had a big CD and vinyl collection of all sorts of music but mainly sixties and seventies rock. One of her all-time favourites was Rory Gallagher who she had told Sadie was a legendary Irish rock guitarist. According to Aunt Suzi, a new collection of his music had just been released. Sadie had decided to surprise her with the CD as a special birthday present. Normally she would have ordered the gift online but she hadn't time as it was so close to her aunt's birthday. Sadie was browsing the rather sparse CD collection in SaveALot when she heard a voice behind her.

'Looking for anything in particular?' Sadie turned to be confronted by Gerry. She had been so engrossed in her task that she hadn't seen him approaching. Automatically, her hand went up to her mask to check that it was in place. She was reassured by its presence and explained what she was looking for.

'Mmm, unfortunately I think SaveALot only stock the more mainstream stuff but, I tell you what, my mate's got a music shop at the back of

The Precinct. If anyone has it round here, he will. I'll give him a call for you if you like when I'm on my break and text you back if you give me your number.' He searched in his pocket and produced his mobile.

Sadie was surprised and pleased. She happily supplied her number and Gerry keyed it into his phone.

'Text you later,' he said. 'By the way, what's your name? I'm Gerry.' He pointed to his name badge.

Sadie smiled. 'Yes, thanks Gerry. I'm Sadie and it's extremely kind of you to go to all this trouble.'

Gerry gave a small salute. 'No trouble at all ma'am. Text you later,' he said before hurrying away.

Sadie guessed that he would be in trouble if he was caught asking a customer for their phone number and recommending another retailer for goods. She realised that a line had now been crossed. Gerry was definitely interested in her. His eyes had lit up when she had readily supplied her phone number. He was so nice. She had often found good-looking men to be over-confident and condescending, but he had a lovely manner and spoke to her as though she was the most important person in the world.

An hour later she got a text: *Tracked it down, Sadie. Seeing my mate later. Could get CD and meet up with you in Precinct Café. They have tables outside so we could socially distance ha ha. If OK with you could meet at seven or another time if not convenient. Let me know. Gerry x*

Well, thought Sadie, as she responded to the text, telling him that seven was fine, it was now or never. She could not imagine that Gerry would be interested in her once she had removed the mask. It would be nice to meet up with him though and an additional positive was that she could get the CD for Aunt Suzi. She had to meet up with him anyway. She owed him the money for the CD. It wasn't as though it was a date really. Perhaps they could have a platonic friendship. She just hoped that their meeting didn't become an anecdote that he would entertain his friends with along the lines of "I met this girl, I thought she was really fit. Trouble is with the lockdown I'd not seen her without a mask. When she took it off, what a shock". No, he seemed nicer than that. Anyway, she was reading too much into the whole situation. But she was going to make sure she looked her best for the meeting. She washed her long dark hair, made her face up carefully and put on her most flattering black jeans, purple linen jacket and best suede boots with little kitten heels.

'Sadie, over here,' Gerry shouted. He was standing outside the café waving excitedly. Sadie thought he looked really nice – even better now he wasn't wearing the SaveALot uniform. He was wearing a great pair of slim fitting light grey jeans, a sparkling white tee-shirt and a dark grey leather jacket. 'Shall we sit here?' he motioned to one of the outside tables. 'Now what can I get you to drink? Wine, beer, coffee?'

'Gerry, I'm going to get you a drink as a thank you for all the trouble you've gone to with the CD,' said Sadie.

Actually, she rather liked the idea of getting the drinks. It meant she had a good excuse for hanging onto the mask for a little longer. 'Would you like a beer? I think I'm going to have one.' Gerry enthusiastically agreed that he would, and Sadie went inside to the bar.

'So,' said Gerry, as Sadie handed him a brimming pint glass, 'I think we're OK to take our masks off now. Moment of truth,' he said and laughed. He seemed a bit embarrassed.

Sadie wondered if he had guessed her secret. Ah well, she could not put the moment off any longer she thought as she unhooked her mask. She was tempted to lighten the situation by saying, 'who *nose* what lies beneath,' but Gerry had already taken his mask off and was looking at her nervously.

'Might as well get it over with,' he said, giving an enormous grin and revealing a mouthful of huge, rather crooked teeth.

As Sadie and Gerry walked away from The Precinct, a couple of hours later, they only had eyes for each other. Time had flown and conversation between them had flowed easily. They had found that they shared a similar outlook on life and enjoyed many of the same things, books, music, and offbeat comedy.

'I didn't think I'd stand a chance with you once you'd seen my enormous gnashers,' confessed Gerry. 'Are you sure you're not put off by them?'

'Gerry, I think they make you look sort of cute,' responded Sadie. 'But my nose, now that's something else.'

Gerry looked confused. 'I haven't noticed that there's anything wrong with it,' he said. 'I think you're really beautiful, exotic-looking somehow and different to any girl I've ever met before. Please, please don't go changing anything. You know one good thing has come out of this dreadful virus situation. Without my mask, I'd never have had the courage to ask you out.'

He squeezed her hand and Sadie felt very happy. As they walked past a shop window she glimpsed their reflection – two happy, smiling young people, brimming with confidence.

# AFTERWORD

I hope you enjoyed this selection of short stories. If so, you may be interested in finding out more about my other publications.

Please do visit my website www.suzihayward.weebly.com for more information and contact details. I always welcome feedback.

*Suzi x*

# ABOUT THE AUTHOR

## Suzi Hayward

Since her retirement, after many years of very varied work experience within the public, private and voluntary sectors, Suzi has been able to indulge her passions for producing and presenting radio shows and developing her creative writing skills.

Over the last eight years, whilst volunteering on community radio stations, she has written, produced and presented numerous programmes and also written and recorded short stories, plays and a radio serial.

One of the student winners of the Hammond House International Literary Competition 2023 and writer of a Screen Yorkshire Connected Campus Short Film of the Month in March 2023, Suzi has had five short stories and a number of articles published in local and national magazines. She is currently completing a BA (Hons) Professional and Creative Writing Degree.

Printed in Great Britain
by Amazon